Too Clever By Half

Also by Roderic Jeffries:

Dead Clever
Death Trick
Relatively Dangerous
Almost Murder
Layers of Deceit
Three and One Make Five
Deadly Petard
Unseemly End
Just Deserts
Murder Begets Murder
Troubled Deaths

RODERIC JEFFRIES

Too Clever By Half

An Inspector Alvarez novel

St. Martin's Press
New York

Library of Congress Cataloging-in-Publication Data

Jeffries, Roderic.
    Too clever by half / by Roderic Jeffries.
        p.   cm.
    ISBN 0-312-04987-0
    I. Title.
    PR6060.E43T6   1990
    823'.914—dc20
                                                              90-37317
                                                              CIP

First published in Great Britain by William Collins Sons & Co. Ltd.

First U.S. Edition: October 1990

10 9 8 7 6 5 4 3 2 1

CHAPTER 1

The sharp sunlight was reflected off the surface of the swimming pool to dance in waves across the ceiling; the sitting-room was oppressively hot and stuffy. Yeo-Eaton looked at the blank television screen and thought about the latest video he had been lent, in which, apparently, there were a couple of ripe scenes. He wondered if he'd be allowed to see them or whether Bronwen would fast-forward.

'I think not the Varleys,' she said.

He turned and briefly looked at her as she sat at the small, beautifully proportioned roll-top desk. Bronwen meant white-breasted, so it was ironic that she should have been christened thus since she regarded such specific anatomical references as disgusting.

'Well?' she said impatiently. 'Don't you agree?'

He jerked his thoughts back to immediate matters. 'Agree, dear?'

'It would help if you'd pay some attention when I speak to you.'

'Of course, dear. Sorry.' He needed a drink, but she believed very firmly that a gentleman did not drink before six-thirty in the evening. Alcohol and sex, she was fond of saying, were the Devil's advocates. He wondered why it was that the Devil enjoyed all the good things in life.

'You agree that we do not invite the Varleys?'

'But I thought you got on with them quite well?'

She had thin lips and when she pursed them, they tended to disappear; her refined voice sharpened from exasperation. 'You know as well as I do that there are people to whom one is pleasant yet whom one doesn't wish to entertain in one's home.'

'He plays a good round of golf.'

'That ceased to be the mark of a gentleman the day they allowed professionals into the club house.'

'But the Varleys do a tremendous amount for the community. They even helped pay most of the fare back to the UK for that couple who hadn't enough money.'

'She sometimes drops her aitches.'

He visualized Hilda Varley. Generously built in all the right places, curly blonde hair topping a round face, and moist lips which promised what her brown eyes suggested. He doubted that she developed many headaches when it was time to go to bed . . .

From the hall came the sound of high-heeled shoes on the tiled floor and Victoria appeared in the doorway. 'I finish,' she said in her fractured English. 'I go.'

Bronwen inclined her head. He said: 'Goodbye, see you tomorrow.'

'Adios, señor.' Victoria flashed him a smile.

He watched her disappear out of sight. She was at the stage, reached early by most Mallorquin women, when beauty had matured to the point where it was teetering towards overripeness. When Bronwen was not present to censor his thoughts, he sometimes fantasized and endowed her with a sharp passion for a retired colonel who had been a dashing subaltern before he'd married his colonel's daughter . . .

'Not the Varleys.' She crossed out the name on the list. She had inherited the desk from a great-aunt who had been Vicereine of India. He had once translated such rank as vice queen. She had expressed sharp displeasure at such stupidity. She used a lace-edged handkerchief to wipe the glow from her forehead (horses sweated, men perspired, ladies merely glowed). 'When on earth is the engineer coming to mend the air-conditioning? Didn't you tell him it was urgent?'

'I said we were nearly expiring from the heat. He promised

to come as soon as possible, but apparently he's a tremendous amount of work in hand.'

'A mere excuse. I should have spoken to him.'

He didn't resent the inference, accepting that it was true. She spoke no Spanish, let alone Mallorquin, yet she possessed the ability to get things done even on the island. A natural sergeant-major of an officer.

She returned her attention to the guest list. 'I suppose we do have to ask Phillipa, even though she never returns hospitality.'

'That's because she can't afford to.'

'Then she should not accept it.'

He knew that it was not Phillipa's poverty to which Bronwen objected, but the fact that she was a woman of marked character, ever ready to speak her mind. She was one of the few people whom Bronwen did not treat with condescension.

'So, with Gerald, that makes thirty-two people.'

He said, surprised: 'D'you mean Gerald Heal?'

'I wasn't aware that we knew any other Geralds.'

'No, we don't. But I thought . . . I rather imagined . . .'

'Do try not to bumble.'

'Yes, dear.'

She closed up the desk and automatically looked around the large, oblong room to make certain that everything was exactly in its place. Clean and tidy in person, clean and tidy in mind. Satisfied, she walked across to the settee and sat. 'Why are you surprised that I'm asking Gerald?'

'Well, it's not all that long ago that you called him distinctly NOCD.'

'He is of the vulgus, obviously, but one can hardly blame him for his unfortunate background.'

'But earlier you said that you wouldn't ask the Varleys because—'

'Godfrey, why do you always have to argue about everything?'

He knew that if he wished to avoid her sharp, bitchy displeasure for the rest of the evening, he should not pursue the matter, but a sudden sense of recklessness made him say: 'You won't ask the Varleys because they're brash, never mind how much good they do among the community, so surely even less should you be ready to ask Gerald, who can be a lot brasher and almost certainly has never done any good to anyone but himself.'

'You don't see the difference?'

'No, I'm afraid I don't.'

'Then it's hopeless trying to explain. There are times when it's quite impossible to talk sense with you.'

As he stared through a window at the pool, the lawn, the lantana hedge, and the mountains, he remembered a brief conversation he'd once heard between two of his subalterns. 'Have you asked him?'— 'Not yet.'— 'Why the hell not?'— 'Because every time I've seen him, Charlotte Corday's been there.' He savoured the memory, even though there'd been no certainty that he and Bronwen had been the two concerned.

'By the way,' she said, 'Ruth rang while you were down in the village collecting the paper.'

'How is she?'

'All right,' she answered.

Even after so many years, he could still be saddened by Bronwen's lack of maternal affection. Just as he could still be amazed by their daughter: first since her presence on earth had called for certain acts of a physical nature; secondly because she had so warm and caring a nature. Ironically, she'd undoubtedly have led a far happier life if her character had been slightly less warm and loving and far more like her mother's. She concerned herself too much with the inadequacies and misfortunes of others and as a result was usually suffering from badly bruised emotions. She had been married once and had later lived with a man—Bronwen had never learned about this—and both relationships had ended disastrously.

Bronwen said: 'I've told her to come a week earlier than she was planning.'

'Then that means she'll be out in just under a fortnight's time.' His pleasure was immediate.

'She wanted to bring some friend, but I said it would be much the best if she came on her own. One never knows how extraordinary her friends will turn out to be.' She paused, then continued: 'I'm quite breathless down here so I'm going up to our bedroom for a while. You did remember to switch on the air-conditioning earlier?'

'Yes, dear.'

As she stood, so did he. His manners were as old-fashioned as his sense of duty. He believed that a man should honour his wife until death relieved him of that burden.

As soon as he heard her climbing the stairs, he crossed to the tall, heavily inlaid cocktail cabinet and poured himself out a very strong whisky, then went through to the kitchen and picked out three ice cubes from the dispenser in the refrigerator. Back in the sitting-room, he sprawled out in a chair and drank, his pleasure all the sweeter because it was not yet quite six o'clock.

He thought how odd it was that Bronwen should have suggested Ruth came out to the island a week earlier, since normally she liked arrangements to be strictly adhered to. Another odd suggestion of hers had been to invite Gerald Heal to their forthcoming cocktail party since it was only recently that she had referred to him as the complete cad. Was she beginning to learn a little flexibility? Not if the Varleys were anything to go by . . . Good God! Of course! Ruth had been ordered to arrive a week earlier in order to be at the cocktail party and Gerald was being invited because, so local rumour had it, he was divorcing his wife. What a ridiculously impossible idea! Gerald Heal wouldn't look twice at a plain, often awkward woman; and in any case, Ruth would have no truck with him because wealth never blinded her to a man's failings; only his inadequacies did that.

CHAPTER 2

'Can't I move?' asked Alma.

'No,' Guy Selby replied.

'But I'm getting pins and needles and I'm sweating like a pig and dying of thirst.'

'Do pigs sweat?'

'I don't know, I don't care, and I'm damned well going to move.' She unfolded her right leg and rubbed the inside of her thigh. 'God, you need a contortionist.'

'Find one who'll keep still for more than two seconds at a time and I'll be happy. Provided she's a body like yours.'

'Your only interest is in my body?'

'Of course.'

'You're a swine.'

'Why not? You're sweating like a pig.'

She stood and stretched. 'I'm not only dying of thirst, I'm starving. Where shall we go for lunch?'

He pointed his brush at her. 'Are you reckoning to eat like that?' She was naked.

'Why not?'

'Mallorquins are conservative. They've only just got used to skinny sunbathing and skinny eating would really throw them.'

'Check with the waiters; you'd find them willing enough to be thrown . . . How's the painting coming along?'

'Lousy.'

She threaded her way between the furniture and piles of books, magazines and general mess on the floor until she could study the canvas on the easel. After a while she said:

'I can never make out whether you denigrate your own work because you're over-modest or are fishing for compliments.'

'Think the worse.'

'You say you're not very good at the human figure and need to practise and practise, yet this is really great.'

'Before you let your enthusiasm overwhelm your critical faculties, you do realize that it's not finished yet, don't you?'

'Of course I do, you idiot . . . You seem to have endowed me with some quality I can't identify. What is it?' She studied his face—rugged, expressing determination and some bloody-mindedness—and knew before he spoke that he was going to answer facetiously.

'Heat, hunger, thirst, and cramp.' He cleaned one brush in a pot, dried it on a square of linen. Six feet one tall and broad-shouldered, his chest bronzed by the sun, there was little of the stereotyped artist in his appearance.

'Be serious,' she begged.

'You're wondering if you remembered to take the Pill and are beginning to panic.'

'You're bloody impossible! Why can't you sometimes admit to being sentimental and not always trying to hide your emotions behind cheap cynicism?'

He cleaned a second brush, then the palette—he was obsessively tidy in his painting, carelessly untidy in the rest of his life. 'Haven't you yet learned the most important fact in life? Whenever you get starry-eyed, you tread on a banana skin.'

'Life can't always have been that tough for you.'

'The consumer society is only fun for people with plenty of money to spend.'

'You can't tell me you'd really like to be a yuppie, for God's sake.'

'Wouldn't I? In my Porsche, driving back to my Docklands pad, my only worry which restaurant to take which girlfriend to? Wouldn't I sell my artistic soul for material wealth after I've spent a humiliating hour trying to interest a gallery owner and he's been yawning away because for him I'm just another slob who's stupid enough to think his daubs are the new van Goghs?'

She said earnestly: 'You must know that with your talent you have to be successful.'

'Cue for the heavenly choir.'

'Go to hell!'

'My lovely dryad, do you really believe that ability always triumphs over indifference and ignorance?'

'Yes.'

'Then I salute you as the last remaining innocent on earth.'

'Can't you ever be optimistic about the future?'

'Right now, I'm very optimistic about the immediate future.'

'You've stopped thinking about painting. I'd better go and dress.'

'Scared? Are you so nervous because you're a virgin?'

'Gallup poll your own sex life, not mine.'

'But yours is so much more interesting.'

'Not for me, I'm hungry. So let's get ready and go out to eat.'

His tone changed. 'I'd rather eat here.' He began to pack tubes of paint into a metal box.

'On what? The fridge is about as bare as Old Mother Hubbard's cupboard.'

'So I'll nip out and buy a barra and some cheese.'

'We are going to Ca'n Toni for lunch.'

'I'd rather—'

'With gentlemanly grace—and I'll explain the term— you're going to agree to do what I want to do, for once.'

The triangular-shaped area to the south of the island was known as La Cuña and it was unusual in two respects— although its longest side was coastline, very few tourists visited it and there was not a single tourist hotel, bar, or restaurant. This absence of tourism was partially because the land was virtually featureless (being so poor it was covered in scrub), but far more importantly because there were no beaches, only cliffs, up to a hundred and fifty metres high, which plunged into the sea.

Of the two villages within La Cuña, Costanyi was the larger. Inevitably, there had been changes there within the past fifty years, since the ripples of prosperity reached everywhere, but compared to other parts of the island, here time had stood still. Ca'n Toni had no sign to mark it as a restaurant, the windows were small and allowed very little light inside, the wooden tables looked as if they must be almost as old as the building, even in summer much of the cooking was done on an open fire in one corner of the room, and the verbal menu offered few dishes.

The waiter—he had only one eye and two fingers on his left hand due to an accident in a quarry—told them the menu and then waited, his expression suggesting a total disinterest.

'I'm going to have shoulder of lamb,' Alma said. 'The same for you?'

Selby shook his head. 'I'll have frito Mallorquin.'

'But you've always said that you reckon the shoulder of lamb here is absolutely delicious.'

'I'm not hungry.'

'What you really mean is, you're too proud to eat what you'd like.'

'Goddamnit—'

'I know. I've been told before that I can't be taken anywhere because I never know when to keep my big mouth shut . . . Guy, this is meant to be a treat for the two of us. Don't spoil it, please.'

He scowled, muttered something unintelligible, then in easy, if ungrammatical Spanish, asked the waiter for two shoulders of lamb and vino corriente. The waiter, who never spoke unless obliged to do so, nodded, left.

She reached across the table and put her hand on Selby's. 'When one of your paintings becomes the star attraction at a Christie's sale, you can treat me to a meal at the Four Seasons.'

'Don't start working up an appetite for the next ninety-five years.'

'I expect to gorge myself at your expense before I'm twenty-five.' In all other respects self-confident to the point of cockiness, when it came to his work he suffered a seemingly endless succession of doubts and she presumed that these were responsible for his many black moods. 'You are going to become very, very famous. People will fall over themselves to buy your paintings.'

'And break their necks before they sign the cheques.'

The waiter returned to place on the table two glass tumblers, an earthenware jug of wine, a small plateful of olives and a larger one on which were slices of pan Mallorquin.

Selby filled the glasses, passed one across. He made an effort to lighten his mood. 'All right, let's drink to the day the hammer drops on the first million-pound Selby.'

The wine, locally made, was harsh and earthy; the olives, locally grown and cured, were bitter. She had learned to enjoy both and as she dropped an olive stone into the wooden ashtray in the centre of the table, she said: 'Gerry was in a good mood at breakfast, so I talked about you.'

'That must have put him off his imported muesli.' Try as he did, he could not mask his sudden sense of resentment. 'Why the hell d'you do that?'

'To try to help you.'

'When I want helping, I'll ask.'

'Bad-temperedly . . . He's in a position to do something for you, so why not find out if he will?'

'Kowtow to the mighty dollar, yen, or whatever currency he's in at the moment.'

She laughed.

'What's so funny?'

'The thought of you kowtowing.'

Reluctantly, he smiled. 'I ought to be good at it. I've spent enough time banging my head against brick walls.'

'You've actually laughed at yourself! Have another glass of wine and who knows what will happen.'

'I'll leave on all fours.'

'Kowtowing all the way . . . I showed Gerry that painting you gave me. He says you're talented.'

'Then there's no further argument. Move over, Leonardo.'

'Sarcasm is not only the lowest form of wit, it also identifies a limited mind. Just because Gerry is stinking rich, it doesn't mean he's an artistic moron. In fact . . .'

'Well?'

She was silent for a while longer, then she said: 'He's a strange man—almost seems to be two people sometimes. He wants people's envy and often spends money merely to prove his wealth, yet there are times when he does something that only a person of real taste could do.'

'You mean he decides not to gild the cold water bath taps as well as the hot?'

'He recognizes beauty where others have failed to do so. Some years ago he was browsing around in an antique shop in Hastings which specialized in paintings and one of these, so dark from varnish and dirt that the subject was only just discernible, caught his attention. Nine hundred and ninety-nine people would have looked at it and decided it was worth only what the frame would fetch; he was the thousandth and he saw something which made him buy it. He had it cleaned and examined by an expert and it turned out to be by a reasonably well known Dutchman who lived part of his life in England at the time of Charles the First; some name like Myens.'

'Daniel Mytens?'

'That's right. Well, the whole point of all this is that he'd never heard of a painter by the name of Mytens and if you put a Mytens next to a van Dyck the chances are he couldn't identify which was which, but he saw in that dirty, indistinct painting something which told him that it was of a totally different quality from all the others. He couldn't begin to define how he knew, he just did. Something in him responds to quality. So when he says you're talented, you damned well are!'

'Who am I to argue any further? But so what?'

'So we are going to persuade him financially to back an exhibition of your work.'

Selby could not contain the excitement such a prospect engendered. 'You think he really might do that?'

'Provided the idea is presented attractively.'

'We tell him he'll be a noble, perhaps eventually ennobled, patron of the arts?'

She smiled briefly. 'Very much more to the point, that he'll make a profit.'

He finished the wine in his glass, refilled both their glasses to empty the jug. 'But hell, even if every painting were to sell, the profit he'd see wouldn't be any more than loose change to him.'

'It's not how much he stands to make that'll attract him, it'll be the fact that he'll make it riding on your back. If you can take advantage of someone, you've proved that you're the smarter.'

He sat back, glass in his right hand. 'You've a funny way of talking about your old man. D'you hate him?'

'D'you know, I've often wondered that.' She rested her elbows on the table, her chin on her hands, and stared into space. 'But the only answer I've ever come up with is, I just don't know. I certainly loathed him every time he chased after a fresh woman and made my mother's life such hell that in the end she left him; he's never seemed to give a damn about me or what I'm doing; and yet I come here to see him from time to time because in spite of everything I recognize a bond between us and I don't think there could be that if I really hated him.'

'There could if your subconscious demanded belief in such a bond because you couldn't face the truth that you do hate your own father.'

'Goddamn it!' She spoke angrily. 'You love digging the knife deep and making me uncertain of myself, don't you?'

'Maybe I'm trying to discover the real you.'

'Why?'

'To see if I'm painting the truth.'

'Has no one ever told you that sometimes a lie can be kinder than the truth?'

CHAPTER 3

Phillipa came to a halt and used the handkerchief, tucked into the short sleeve of her dress, to mop the sweat from her forehead. It was extraordinarily hot for early May but, as she replied whenever asked about what weather to expect in Mallorca, the only certainty was uncertainty.

As she rested she stared at the view, which for her never staled. Llueso, centred around the hill on which it had first been built as a defence against the Moors, looked timeless except on the outskirts, where modern boxy blocks of flats had been built; the hermitage on Puig Antonia to the south, if no longer housing hermits because solitude and self-denial had ceased to attract, still reached up to heaven; the farmland was good, though not as rich as that around nearby Mestara, and crops were heavy; the bay, ringed by mountains, remained as beautiful as ever because from where she stood the development around it was hidden . . . Development. The cancer of the island. Right then, she could hear a concrete mixer turning and a pneumatic rock-breaker at its even noisier work. Llueso council had imposed a total ban on all new building because even they had dimly realized that with each extra house or block of flats a little more of the peace and beauty was lost, but no one paid the slightest attention to their edict. She'd first come to the island so long ago that she could remember when beyond Palma the roads were dirt and hardly a foreigner was to be seen; when to reach the new Parelona Hotel, one had to travel to Parelona Bay by boat because there was only a mule track over the mountainous promontory; when the Mallorquins had been a kind, contented people whom one could trust in everything . . . She shook her head. She was old. Had things really been as perfect as she now remembered them, or was she forgetting what she wished to forget? She could no longer be certain. People said that age brought compensations. She was damned if she'd discovered any.

She resumed her walk up the gently rising road which eventually led into Festna Valley. On either side were metre-high stone walls which trapped and reflected the heat, and as the sweat rolled down her face and back she could feel her heart beat more quickly than was welcome. She should have forgone a second brandy after her meal.

She passed a house recently reformed, in front of which had been built a large swimming pool. Foreigners who rented houses in the summer now demanded pools and so dozens had recently been installed; every pool lost a lot of water through evaporation and this had to be replaced; the greatly increased consumption of water from that and other causes was lowering the water-table, with the consequence that in the height of summer the water to Llueso was turned off throughout the day, leaving the locals resentfully waterless because the tourists in the port must not go short, while in the port most of the wells were being contaminated with salt water . . . Yet still the development continued.

The road became more level, making walking easier. The

journey was too short to warrant her using her very old Seat 600 and normally she would not have made it until the evening had brought cooler conditions; but when she'd rung Justin, he had not answered the call and she was very worried that something had happened to him.

She came abreast of another gateway and in the field beyond, weeding between recently transplanted aubergines, was a woman dressed in a shapeless frock and a wide-brimmed straw hat. There was at least one aspect of island life which hadn't changed despite all the development, Phillipa thought; the women worked in the fields whilst the men talked in the bars. She called out: 'Antonia.'

Antonia, her face bronzed by the sun despite invariably wearing a hat, slowly straightened up. 'Good afternoon, señorita.'

'How's your leg now?' If asked, Phillipa always claimed to be a fluent Castilian and a reasonable Mallorquin speaker; in fact, her Castilian was heavily accented and frequently grammatically faulty and her Mallorquin raised smiles behind her back.

'It's healing very slowly, señorita. I saw the doctor yesterday afternoon and told him it was still hurting and he said that it must do after so deep a cut.'

'You should rest it more.'

'How, when there is work to do?'

'By telling García to do it instead of chatting to Ramón.' When she had first come to the island, the ordinary people had been poor and virtually illiterate and it had seemed reasonable to speak to them with an inquisitive, condescending authority. Antonia's generation still accepted this arrogance without any resentment, but the younger people did not; Phillipa would have been deeply upset to learn how much ill-feeling she often caused. 'And tell García that just before lunch his beastly goat ate one of my special geraniums.'

'How terrible, señorita!'

'The seeds cost a thousand pesetas.' It was her contention
that the only way in which to bring home to a Mallorquin
the seriousness of any situation was to present it in financial
terms. 'And I told him only yesterday that that fence would
never keep a goat back for five minutes if it decided to try
to get out.'

'But all the goats were hobbled.'

'Since when has hobbling kept a determined goat from
wandering? You tell that husband of yours that he must put
up a much stronger and higher fence. If his beastly animals
eat any more of my special geraniums, I'll make him pay
for new seeds.'

'He'll do that, never fear.'

Phillipa walked on. It was unlikely the fence would be
strengthened. Either Antonia would forget to pass on the
message, or García would agree to do it and minutes later
forget what it was he had agreed. Mañana was as much
about forgetfulness as deliberate evasion.

She reached the house that her brother, like her, rented
on a life lease. It was considerably larger than hers and
possessed over fifteen hundred square metres of land in
which grew orange and lemon trees and one very large fig
tree whose fruit was small and really only suitable for drying
and feeding to animals. Justin Burnett was no gardener and
the few rose-bushes were losing their fight against a host of
weeds, but the bright red bougainvillæa seemed to thrive
on neglect and one wall was aflame with the bracts.

She opened the front door, stepped into the entrada.
'Justin . . . Justin, are you all right?' she shouted. She tried
to recall the doctor's name and couldn't because of an
increasing tension.

Then there was a shout from upstairs. 'What's the matter?'

'I telephoned and there was no answer.'

'For God's sake!'

She went into the sitting-room. Around the walls Justin

had had shelves fixed and on these were the books which had been in their father's library; also present was their father's desk. To sit surrounded by such things was to be reminded of the library in their old home, an evocation that was both sweet and bitter; sweet because of the hours spent listening to him reading from the classics, bitter because it had been there that they'd first learned of their father's financial loss and the probable consequences of this . . .

Justin, dressed in open-neck shirt and shorts, his sparse hair in disarray, came slowly down the stairs and into the sitting-room. 'For God's sake, what's brought you here in siesta-time?' he asked in his high-pitched, querulous voice.

'I've just told you. I phoned to see how you were and you didn't answer.' He was ageing very, very rapidly, she thought. His long face had always been thin, but now the skin was sinking to make it look skeletal; when he had arrived on the island, he had been able to conceal any baldness by growing his hair long, now that was impossible; once he'd walked with an upright carriage, now his shoulders were bowed. 'You had me really worried. Couldn't you see I would be?'

'Since I didn't know it was you phoning, how could I?'

'Who else would it have been at that time?'

He sat heavily in the second armchair.

'You might have—'

He interrupted her roughly. 'When my head was pounding like a bloody steam engine, I wasn't concerned who it was.'

Her resentment turned to fresh worry. 'Again? But it's only a couple of days since you last had a terrible headache.'

'D'you think I don't know that?'

'You must go back and see the specialist again . . .'

'He can't tell me anything I don't already know.'

'Don't you think . . .'

'For God's sake, stop bothering me.'

Her lips tightened, but she did not reply. She had been brought up in a family in which the men had had to be honoured and humoured and she still accepted that responsibility, even though she was by far the stronger character. When their father had lost his money through unwise investments, it had been she who had faced up to the consequences while Justin had desperately tried to insulate himself from reality; it had been she who had first gone out to work, braving a world for which their upbringing had not prepared them, while for months afterwards he had remained at home, too frightened and resentful to follow her example . . . She spoke, trying to force him out of his present black mood. 'One of García's goats broke into my garden and ate one of those special geraniums.'

He might not have heard.

'I told him that the fence he'd put up wouldn't hold the goats, but he wouldn't listen.'

'They're all stupid.'

'Stubborn rather than stupid.' To others, even her brother, she always defended the Mallorquins and it was only to herself that she admitted that the truth was that they so often behaved stupidly because they were seemingly incapable of foreseeing trouble.

'Lydia called this morning,' he said.

'That was nice.'

'It wasn't. My head had started and she insisted on going on and on about that family of hers.'

'She's very proud of them.'

'Why can't she be very proud of them somewhere else? Why should I suffer just because Vernon's got an IQ in four figures?'

'His name's Redmund; Vernon's the Praters' son.'

'What's it matter what his name is?'

'He's expected to get a very good degree.'

'By cheating, no doubt.'

'Justin, I wish you'd go back and see the specialist again.'

'All he can say is, I should have the operation. I won't. D'you understand, I won't.'

'It might not be nearly as bad as you fear. D'you remember Tony? He came through the operation wonderfully well . . .'

'I don't give a damn if he enjoyed a resurrection. I'm not going to have it and that's that.'

She could not quite erase the word 'coward' from her mind. 'Would you like some coffee?'

'No.'

'I would, so if I make some, will you drink a cup?'

'You think coffee's going to clear my head?'

'It might make you feel a little better.'

'You can be incredibly stupid.'

She only just stopped herself from finally delivering a very tart rejoinder. She stood. 'I'll make enough so that if you change your mind there'll be a cupful for you.'

The kitchen was very much better equipped than hers and instead of a laboriously hand-operated coffee-grinder, he had an electric one that reduced beans to near powder in seconds. She opened a cupboard, to bring out the coffee-maker, and discovered that he'd bought himself an electric percolator. He'd always been of an extravagant nature . . . Disloyalty, she told herself, was the eighth deadly sin. If he could afford to buy a new coffee-maker, why shouldn't he? It wasn't as if he didn't help her quite often financially . . . Groundless resentment was the ninth deadly sin. She'd no right to wonder why he, the weakling, should have ended up with a substantial career pension, fully index-linked, while she, because of misfortunes quite beyond her control, had only a small, non-index-linked pension to supplement her state one . . .

The coffee made, she poured it into the silver coffee jug which had come from their mother's family, searched for the matching milk jug before she remembered that recently he had dropped and damaged it. Naturally, the son had inherited all the silver. But if the milk jug had been hers and it had been damaged, she would never have just put it into a drawer and forgotten it, not caring enough to find out if it could be mended locally.

CHAPTER 4

When Gerald Heal had bought the property, it had been called Son Temor; having little time for history and none for modesty, he had renamed it Ca'n Heal. It was a manor house, imposingly large, set at the head of a long, wide valley. Originally, all the valley had been owned, but now the holding was reduced to just over two hectares. Close to the range of outbuildings was a large well with an almost limitless capacity even in midsummer, so that there was far more water than was needed; the farmers who now owned the surrounding land had wanted Heal to sell them the surplus water, but he had refused. What was his, was his.

The square house, four floors high, was built around an inner courtyard. In this, he had had built a stone fountain and now no matter how stifling the heat, the courtyard was a place of musical coolness. The house had been unreformed, so he had engaged an architect from Madrid to modernize it. The architect had been a man of vision and taste, very generous with other people's money. When Heal had added up what the reformation had cost, he had been shocked and ever afterwards referred to 'that swindler of an architect'. But since the work was of a quality rarely met on the island and there was extra envy to be gained from being so rich that one could be that handsomely cheated (he hadn't been; on the whole, Madrileño architects, unlike many local ones, were both conscientious and honest), his resentment wasn't as great as his words suggested.

He had filled the house with valuable possessions. Most had been bought on the open market but some, like the Mytens painting, he had acquired at a fraction of their true value because of his gift of being able to discern the beauty of genius. Those possessions bought in the open market were often so ostentatiously impressive as to be ugly, but all his 'finds' were truly beautiful. There was here a dichotomy of character almost impossible to understand until one knew and understood his past.

He had been born into bastardy and considerable hardship, if not quite poverty. That bastardy was an unfortunate condition was first truly brought home to him after two older boys had enjoyed themselves immensely, beating him up on the grounds that as a bastard he was a polluting influence. The tears he had shed had been tears of humiliation as much as of pain and this humiliation, which he never learned to forget, had been responsible for firing him with a burning ambition to prove himself a lot smarter and tougher than all those lucky enough to have been born with two parents and in some comfort.

He'd made his first million by his twenty-fifth birthday, nine years after starting full-time work in a builder's yard in Camberwell. By the time he was forty he was worth, on a conservative estimate, ten million. Unlike most other rich people, he saw money not as power, but as a means of buying admiration and envy and so he retired rather than continue to work at making still more money which he'd never have the time, or eventually the ability, to spend with profit to himself.

He'd naturally had no intention of allowing any government to tax him and then waste his money on half-baked social schemes, so he'd moved all his capital out of England and into a bank in Jersey and from there to a company in Switzerland which invested it through a company in Liechtenstein. His Liechtenstein company bought the house and he was their tenant. Since the Spanish government

had made the mistake of introducing a modern system of
taxation which caught anyone who lived in the country for
more than five months and thirty days, he made certain it
could not be proved that he did. He paid most bills on credit
cards whose accounts were settled in the States in dollars
and he drew cash through cashpoints since their records of
withdrawals were not kept locally; no snooping Spaniard
was ever going to find it easy to prove that he was liable to
pay Spanish income tax. As a Rothschild had once said, a
rich man didn't necessarily have to be a fool.

The company employed five servants, three in the house
and two in the garden; the house was always spick and
span, the garden a blaze of colour. He treated them fairly,
but did not allow them the slightest familiarity, as did so
many expatriates. All men weren't equal, not by many bank
balances.

He was tall, well built, had broad shoulders and a slim
waist; many women thought him handsome. He was quick-
witted, intelligent, and possessed a humour which could
match itself to his listeners. Introduced to three strangers
at a cocktail party, within minutes they would be listening
to him rather than to each other. Most people liked him on
first acquaintance and it was only the confirmed snobs, or
the very perspicacious, who saw in his moustache an accurate indication of character. One of his many women, locked
out of his 'love' flat for no reason other than boredom with
her, had labelled him a barrow-boy made good. It was
difficult to think of an apter description.

Alma stepped from the vast entrance hall into the snuggery—the small sitting-room which he used when not entertaining and impressing, in which were television, video and
hi-fi, naturally all of the highest quality. ''Evening, Gerry.'
She treated him as a friend (or enemy), not a father, and
he preferred this because sentiment made him uneasy.

He looked up. 'Your mother rang earlier and wants you
to phone her back immediately.'

'Is something the matter?'

'If there is, it can't be serious because she didn't complain.'

She hated him for this open contempt. It had been his blatant infidelities which had finally brought about the separation. 'D'you mind if I phone her?'

'For God's sake, you don't have to ask.'

If she hadn't, she thought, he might well have complained. There was a phone in the snuggery, but this was a call she did not want overheard. She returned to the entrance hall and crossed to the library. The shelves were filled with leather-bound books and any man who'd read them all could count himself educated. She doubted he'd read any of them. She sat on the edge of the large partner's desk, lifted the receiver, and dialled 07. When the connection with International was made, she dialled 33 for France and then the number. As she waited, she nervously wondered what had happened to make her mother ring through and face having to speak to her husband.

'Who is it?'

Her mother's words sounded slightly slurred; it could be distortion or it could be drink. 'It's Alma. I'm sorry I was out when you rang. Gerry says you want a word?'

'I'm surprised the bastard remembered to tell you.'

She'd never been able to decide in her own mind whether her mother had believed the marriage could last, despite the difference in characters, or whether it had been a simple case of being dazzled by wealth. 'Is something wrong, Mother?'

'I've just had a letter from the bastard's solicitors. And d'you know what they've written . . .'

She listened patiently to a long and involved story, the gist of which she had guessed immediately. Her mother had run out of money, had written to her father's solicitors to ask for more, and had been refused. Her mother spent money with an abandon that was at times breathtaking; for her, financially there was no tomorrow. If she saw a dress

that attracted her, she bought it no matter what the cost
and even though the cupboards in her house were filled
with clothes; another gold bracelet was a necessity for a
well-dressed lady; one never ever drank vin ordinaire, only
château-bottled wine . . .

'You have to tell him.'

'Tell him what?'

'Haven't you been listening to a word I've said? Tell the
bastard that I must have my allowance increased. I can't
go on like this while he's wallowing in luxury. When I think
of what he should be giving me . . .'

Alma leaned across the desk and opened a silver-gilt
cigarette box, brought out a cigarette, lit this with a gold
Dunhill lighter. Drink always exacerbated her mother's
bitterness, resentment, and envy.

'. . . so tell him he must agree to let me have more money.'

'I don't think that that would be a very good idea.'

'Why not?'

'You know how his mind works. Tackle him head on and
he'll refuse. If you really think it's worth your while asking
him, write him a letter and very quietly explain how the
cost of everything keeps going up. And don't be definite
unless you're absolutely certain you're right—you know
how he checks up on things. At the end, just ask him to let
you have a bigger allowance if he can afford to be generous
—he won't want to appear to be unable to afford. Don't
complain, don't moan, and be pleasant.'

'Pleasant to that bastard?'

'Yes, Mother, pleasant. That is, if you really want any
hope of getting your allowance raised . . .'

'Why d'you keep saying "allowance"? It's money he owes
me.'

'I know how you feel about it, but remember what those
solicitors in London said. The marriage has irretrievably
broken down and if you both lived in the UK you'd have a
legal right to a proper share of his assets that could be

enforced. But neither of you lives at home and it's certain that Gerry's transferred all his assets overseas. In such circumstances, it's almost impossible to make certain your rights are enforced. In fact, if he decided to cut you off without another penny, in practical terms there's probably very little you could do about it. And if you annoy him too much, he will cut you off.'

'He's a bastard.'

'So you mentioned.'

'He doesn't care that I'm living in penury.'

'Mother, there are a hell of a lot of people who would like to live in your "penury". If you could cut back on some of your extravagances . . .'

'Extravagances! If I'm so depressed I buy myself a little something to try to cheer myself up, I suppose that's being hopelessly extravagant? Maybe even continuing to live is a hopeless extravagance . . .'

She flicked ash from the cigarette into the silver ashtray that was shaped as a dolphin. She was a go-between. Her mother vented her anger, and Gerry his resentful contempt, through her . . .

'All right, Mother, I'll see how things go and speak to him if the right moment turns up.' It was not a promise that she intended to keep. It was usually safe never to prophesy how Gerald would react, since he delighted in being contrary, but in this instance it was—he would do whatever was likely to hurt his wife the most.

She said goodbye, replaced the receiver, slid off the desk, stubbed out the cigarette and returned to the snuggery. On one of the small coffee tables there was now an ice bucket in which was an opened bottle. 'Champers or something else?' he asked.

'That'll do.'

He smiled. Since she was his daughter, he didn't mind her occasionally mocking his lifestyle. He lifted a tulip-shaped glass from the silver salver and filled it, passed it across.

The champagne was vintage Heidsieck Monopole and

must have cost a fortune, she thought. Even the better Spanish cavas were far cheaper, but he never drank them; probably he'd read somewhere that a man with any pretensions to a palate would rather enjoy one glassful of champagne than suffer ten glassfuls of sparkling white.

'Well, is there a crisis in France?' he asked.

'She wanted a chat, that's all.'

'Something at which she's always been proficient.'

'Among a great number of other things, as you'd have discovered if ever you'd taken the trouble to find out.'

He shrugged his shoulders. He understood Alma's desire to stick up for her mother, without ever accepting that it was justified. 'What kind of a day did you have?'

'Painful. I kept being threatened by cramp, starvation, and death by dehydration, but sympathy was there none. When he's working, Guy's a lesson in selfishness.'

'What kind of painting is it?'

'A full-length study.'

'Yes, but . . .' He refilled his glass. 'Decent?'

'It's certainly not pornographic.'

'Then you are dressed?'

'No, I'm not.'

'Why not?' he demanded sharply.

'Because the object of the exercise is for him to have practice in painting the human form, warts and all.'

'Why doesn't he hire a model?'

'Mallorquin women aren't into nude modelling.'

'I should bloody well think not.'

'Gerry, you're being delightfully Victorian.'

'Because I don't like the thought of my daughter appearing in the nude?'

'A painter sees his model as something to paint, not screw.' She was amused by the hypocrisy not only of her last statement, but also of the whole conversation; Guy's thoughts were often of a non-artistic nature and a moral attitude sat uneasily on her father's shoulders.

'I don't like the idea.'

'Will it make you any happier if I tell you that I won't indulge in a Bohemian life just for the hell of it.'

'I disapprove.'

'Why be a parent if one doesn't disapprove of one's offspring's activities? . . . Gerry, the art critic on *La Vanguardia* saw two or three of Guy's paintings and said they showed tremendous talent.'

'For pleasing dirty old men?'

'He didn't see the Mallorquin Venus. He mentioned a very influential art gallery in Barcelona which is always on the lookout for new talent and he reckoned that the owner would probably give Guy an exhibition. That would really be something, because Barcelona has become a very important centre.'

'Presumably you're telling me this because you want something?'

'You don't think that that's being horribly cynical?'

'You tell me.'

She did not accept the challenge. 'I didn't realize this before, but art's rather like car racing.'

'Surely one of the more recherché comparisons?'

'Not really. If you want to succeed, you have to be known, but in order to be known, you have to succeed. The only short cut through that Catch 22 situation is to find a sponsor who'll make you financially attractive to a team manager. In the same way, if an artist wants to succeed . . .'

'Cutting things short, you're trying to say that Guy wants a sponsor.'

'Who'll put up a relatively small sum of money in the certainty of making a good profit.'

'The certainty being, no doubt, of the same order as that of a Derby favourite?'

'You don't quite understand. I've been checking and the way the galleries in Barcelona work is that either they stage an exhibition entirely at their own cost and take fifty per cent of all sales, or they charge a flat sum which covers all overheads plus, and take either a much lower or no percentage on sales. Obviously, if a painter probably won't make more than a couple of sales, it's in his best interests to work under the first scheme; if he's likely to do well, the second. But to be able to choose the latter, he has to put down the full payment in advance.'

'Which no artist can?'

'Very few, certainly.'

'Guy's not one of the very few.' It was a flat statement of fact, not a question.

'Unfortunately, no.'

'So he thinks I might play the sucker?'

'I've no idea. I naturally haven't discussed the idea with him.'

'Naturally?'

'He has to paddle his own canoe.'

He was perplexed. 'Then why are you telling me all this?'

'Because by my calculations, if Guy had an exhibition where he paid the flat sum and the gallery took either no or very little commission on each sale, the backer would make a handsome profit if half the paintings sold and would double his money if three-quarters did.'

'Where would all this profit come from?'

'In the agreement the backer would be given a percentage on all sales over and above repayment in full.'

'If it's so certain he'll sell well, why doesn't the gallery owner insist on a percentage rather than a flat sum?'

'Because every gallery owner can remember exhibitions which have failed dismally.'

'So now the story returns to earth!'

'Failed because the owner misjudged the value of the work. The history of art is full of people who've misjudged paintings because they didn't have that special something which says whether a painting really is, or is not, truly great. Let's face it, very few people have. But you're one of those

very few. And you said that Guy's work is really good.
Which means that there has to be a strong chance it will
sell well. So you could stand to make a handsome profit for
doing nothing more than relying on your own judgement.'

He drained his glass, refilled it. 'Does he have enough
paintings?'

'It would take some time to set up an exhibition and by
then he would have, yes. Of course, he'd need a loan for
framing, transport, catalogues, and the party on the opening
night. Like you, he's a cynic and he reckons that an artist's
reviews bear a direct relationship to the quality and quantity
of the champagne he serves on his opening night.'

'Any additional loan would have to have the same priority
of repayment as the main one.'

'Of course.'

He drank. After a while he said forcefully: 'I'm not
subsidizing him to show a painting of you in the nude that
grubby little men in raincoats leer at.'

She smiled. 'You really are sweet, Gerry!' She added, in
a conspiratorial tone: 'If you'd put up the money, surely
you'd be able to claim the right to tell him he mustn't
exhibit that painting?'

CHAPTER 5

Bronwen's august, commanding, and pervasive presence
did nothing to make the Yeo-Eatons' cocktail party any
more pleasurable than were other people's. She would not
let events take their natural course, but insisted on her
guests mixing and not staying in tight little circles so that
more often than not she forced together people who disliked
each other; also, being a prude, she made a point of disturbing pleasure and she spoke sharply to two men who were
trying to persuade two ladies to strip off to their underclothes

for a swim in the pool, headed off a couple who had been making for the shadows which lay beyond the lantana hedge, and dragged her husband away from an interesting conversation with a forty-year-old divorcee . . .

Much to Phillipa's annoyance, the Brookers had been shepherded by Bronwen into talking to her.

'The rise in the cost of living, as measured by the price of a bottle of brandy . . .' Brooker gave a neighing laugh. 'The most accurate index of inflation there is, I always say.' He turned to his wife, who had chosen a long dress and was worried because only two other women had done the same. 'That's what I always say, isn't it, dear?'

'Yes, dear.'

'Well, the price of a bottle of brandy has gone up by . . . I'll bet you can't guess?'

'A hundredfold,' replied Phillipa shortly.

'No, no, not quite as bad as that! Although I must admit that it sometimes seems like it . . .'

'When I first came to the island, a bottle of reasonable brandy cost six pesetas.'

'Oh! Is that a fact? Then you must have been here a very long time . . . Well, I was really thinking of the time we've been living here. Things really have shot up in the past three years.' He turned to his wife. 'Haven't they, dear?'

'Yes, dear,' Denise replied.

'The cost of living has shot up everywhere in the civilized world,' said Phillipa.

'But more here, dear lady, at this end of the island. Take the humble vegetable. A lettuce used to cost . . .'

'Dear man, I'm as capable of appreciating the rise in prices as you are.' The unaccustomed amount of champagne she had drunk had made her more aggressive than usual. 'I live on a small pension. In the old days I could afford to eat at a restaurant several times a week, now I'm lucky if it's once a fortnight and I have to be satisfied with the menu del dia.'

'Of course you know what the trouble is, don't you?'

'Do I?'

'They've all become so greedy.'

'And who exactly are "they"?'

'Why, the Mallorquins.'

'Then who's made them greedy? It's the foreigners who come and pay the maids six hundred an hour when they're not worth two hundred because none of them is trained to do anything but break crockery and electrical plugs.'

'But . . . but that's what they're asking in the port.'

'That's right,' said his wife, hoping Phillipa did not know that she paid her maid seven hundred an hour.

'They always ask for more than they expect to get because that's the Arab blood in them. And when they get paid what they ask, they know they're dealing with fools.'

Brooker, his drooping jowls and double chin increasing his resemblance to a turkeycock, said plaintively: 'If they won't come unless you pay them what they ask, there's no alternative.'

'There's an excellent alternative. It's called doing the work oneself.'

Rosa, a cousin of Victoria, who was helping with the service, approached them. Proud of her English, she said: 'You like more?' The lower half of the bottle of champagne was carefully swathed in a serviette to hide the label. The Yeo-Eatons did not wish to embarrass anyone by making it clear that they were serving a cheaper champagne than they normally drank since to do so would underline the truth that their palates were superior to those of most of their guests.

Phillipa held out her glass. 'How's your mother?' she asked in Spanish.

'Much better, thank you, señorita. She went to see a new doctor and he gave her some different pills and her stomach's happier.'

'That's good. And your sister?'

'She has a good job with the bank. Her novio finishes his milly next month and they are to marry in June.'

'Have they a house?'

'José's mother was left one by an aunt and she's given it to them to live in. I'm helping to decorate it.'

'I hope I'm to be invited to the wedding?'

'But of course, señorita. It's unthinkable that you shouldn't be.'

'And to the christening.'

Rosa giggled.

Brooker, who'd been becoming more and more impatient, said: 'I and the wife would like another little drink if that's not too much trouble.'

Rosa hadn't understood the words, but the nature of the request had been unmistakable. She refilled both glasses, which emptied the bottle, and left.

'I wish I could speak Spanish as well as you do,' said Denise ingratiatingly.

'You never will until you try,' retorted Phillipa.

'But I do. My trouble is, I forget the words. And it's all so terribly difficult when things have different genders. I mean, how am I to know if a tree's masculine or feminine?'

Brooker laughed coarsely. 'That's obvious, isn't it? It's masculine . . . What I say is, what's the point in bothering. If they want something from you, they understand English soon enough. Make 'em speak English, that's what I say.'

'You don't surprise me,' said Phillipa. She turned and, careless about such rudeness, walked away. Back in Britain, the Brookers had been no more than prosperous, conventional, small-minded suburbanites, yet on the island they looked down on the Mallorquins with intolerant condescension; condescension that frequently turned to dislike when they were faced with the resentment their attitude bred.

She joined a small group of three, just beyond the steps down into the floodlit pool.

'Hullo, Phillipa,' said Heal. 'You're looking very chic.'

'And you're as big a liar as ever.' She had identified him as a cad at their first meeting, but in her long life had come to the conclusion that, provided one did not have to do business with them, cads were more entertaining than the righteous.

'You know what they say, don't you? A lie a day keeps one rich and gay . . . Gay in the old-fashioned sense, I hasten to add.' He was, as always, a shade too smartly dressed; yachting jacket, silk shirt, linen trousers, and white buckskin shoes.

McColl, in his late sixties, small but without the peppery character of many small men, said: 'It's a great pity "gay" has come to mean a homosexual. It used to have a conno-tation that's difficult to define now. For instance, how can you describe the kind of person we used to call a gay woman?'

'Bubbly?' suggested his wife, built on a generous scale and unworried by the fact.

Heal said: 'Talking about bubbly, let's see if we can get our glasses recharged.' He looked round, saw Victoria, smiled at her and she came across, a bottle in one hand, a plate in the other. She refilled their glasses, but they refused the tired, dispirited canapés.

Conversation was general for a few moments, then McColl looked at his watch and said they ought to be moving because they had to go to another party that evening; his wife made a face, suggesting that had the choice been hers, she would have returned home. They said goodbye, left.

'So are you thinking of going back to England for a holiday?' Heal asked.

'My cousin's daughter has had a baby and I'd like to go to the christening,' replied Phillipa, 'but I can't afford to.'

He hastily turned the conversation away from money;

naturally, being very rich, worried that she might be about to ask him to help her financially. 'Given the alternative of staying here or returning home in order to go goo-goo over a baby, I'd stay here.'

'Of course. You're demonstrably undomesticated, despite having an attractive daughter . . . And incidentally, I haven't seen her this evening? Has she gone back home?'

'She's still with me, but she wasn't invited. I asked if she'd like me to speak to the Yeo-Eatons, who probably don't know she's staying with me, but she said she'd rather enjoy life.'

'Sensible gal.' She drained her glass.

'Phillipa, you know everyone worth knowing. Who's that who's just appeared?'

'Appeared where?'

'Under the covered patio. She's talking to our hostess.'

Phillipa squinted as she tried to focus her gaze more clearly. 'Irma, the Contessa Imbrolie. If that were my name, I'd change it; too close to imbroglio. In any case, Irma Imbrolie is tautologous.'

'What nationality is she?'

'Probably more English than you, since she was born in some place like Wolverhampton. She married an Italian count, which is no difficult feat since in that country counts seem to be two a penny. Her husband died last year, from some sort of stomach trouble. Italians eat far too much pasta.'

'That's a very elegant dress she's wearing.'

'Is it?' She again concentrated her gaze. 'I suppose it is, if you like exaggeration. But in any case, next to Bronwen most dresses look like haute couture.' It wasn't until he chuckled that she realized she needed to control her tongue.

'D'you know her well?'

She spoke more carefully. 'I've met her a couple of times at parties, that's all.'

'She looks good fun.'

'That depends on what meaning you accord "good fun", doesn't it?' She made up her mind; nothing more to drink and so to bed. 'I must be moving.'

'Can I run you back in my car?'

'Thank you, but the walk will do me good.'

She left. As she passed the Contessa Imbrolie, she decided that Heal had been right; probably the dress had come from one of the major Italian or French fashion houses. Rumour had it that the Count had been a very wealthy man; wealthy, but not very sensible, since he'd married a woman so very much younger than himself.

Heal parked his Mercedes 500 alongside the white Ford Fiesta, left the garage and crossed to the west door of the house. When he entered he could hear the music, even though the snuggery was on the other side.

Alma used the remote control to turn down the volume of the CD player. 'How was Bronwen? Noble Roman nose held high?'

'She's not too bad if you don't take her seriously.' He sat in the nearest armchair. 'As a matter of fact, it was quite an enjoyable party.'

She cocked her head slightly to one side as she studied him. 'Praise like that must signify something. Was the booze good or did you meet a tasty dish?'

'You won't credit me with simply a pleasure at being alive?'

'Not unless you've found a way of turning that pleasure into profit.' She switched off the player, stood. 'You may be full of contentment, but I'm quite hungry. You said you wouldn't want a cooked meal after a cocktail party and I'm just as happy with a very light meal, so Carolina's just left out a salad, pâté, cheese, and a homemade spinach coca. How about a couple of eggs on top of a slice of coca?'

'Sounds good.'

'I'll go and do that. Shall we eat here, on our laps—

there's a programme on the local telly I want to watch
which comes on after the news?'

'In Spanish?'

'Of course. I'm managing to understand enough to get
the gist of things.'

'You're a smart girl.'

'A compliment from you? You are in an extraordinarily
good humour! Maybe it's the moment to remind you that
there are only seven months to Christmas.' She laughed.
'Don't panic, I was only joking. Diamonds may be a girl's
best friend, but they've never said very much to me.'

As she left, he settled back in the chair and stretched out
his legs. Diamonds did a lot for the Contessa Imbrolie. The
necklace had looked superb on her. That one piece must
have cost more than all the jewellery the rest of the women
had been wearing . . .

Marriage had its drawbacks—as he could testify—but
there were times when it had something to offer. A couple
were received more often and more willingly than a single
man. A wife could run the house properly and be ever ready
to be a gracious hostess. She stopped malicious suggestions
from small-minded people who professed to see special
significance in a man's liking for sartorial and personal
smartness. Should she have a title, she'd open doors that
would otherwise remain closed. And if in addition she owned
a fortune in her own right, then she could not be marrying
for money . . . Yes, there were many good reasons to think
of marrying again.

CHAPTER 6

Dolores put a bowl of hot chocolate on the kitchen table.
'It's already past nine.'

Alvarez sat down on the stool. 'It's of no account. The

superior chief went off to some conference in Madrid and isn't due back until midday.'

'But I thought you were complaining you'd so much work to do, you didn't know how you'd ever get even half of it done?'

'And I still don't know.' He broke off a piece of ensaimada, dunked it in the chocolate, ate.

'Well, you're not going to discover how all the time you sit here instead of hurrying off to the office, are you?'

'You don't understand.'

'That's just about right. And d'you know why I don't? It's because I'm a woman who has to do ten different jobs every hour and doesn't have the time to worry about how to do them.' She stared challengingly at him, but he merely dunked another piece of ensaimada. She sighed as she turned away and went over to the refrigerator. One could feed a mule oats, but one would never make butter out of its milk.

The phone rang, kept on ringing. 'Well,' she demanded, 'aren't you going to answer?'

'It might not be for me.'

'It might not be for me, but you seem to expect me to go.' Handsome head held high, she left.

He used a handkerchief to wipe the sweat from his forehead and neck. It was extraordinarily hot, even when one remembered that it was now mid-July. Heat sapped the strength from a man and left him good for nothing . . .

She returned to the kitchen. 'The call was for you! The sargento wants a word.'

'What's up?'

'Perhaps you'd like me to go back and find out if it's important enough for you to interrupt your meal?'

Morosely, he dunked a last piece of ensaimada. The sargento was, on the whole, a sensible man and therefore would not have rung this early in the morning had the matter not been urgent. Had the superior chief returned

early from Madrid, rung the post and demanded to speak
to the inspector? It was the kind of sneaky thing that
essentially sneaky man would do. As he finished the chocolate, he mentally composed several excuses for his absence
from the office and tried to decide which was the safest.

He left the kitchen and walked through the dining-
room-cum-living-room into the entrada, which was also the
formal entertaining room and therefore used only on high
days and holidays and kept so scrupulously clean by Dolores
that any speck of dust in it felt lonely. He lifted the receiver.
'Yes?'

'You've finally managed to drag yourself out of bed, then!'
said the sargento.

'I've been down at the port since eight, looking for a
witness.'

'Only in your dreams, you lazy old sod . . . Listen, Enrique. There's been a death in the Huerta. An Englishman
by the name of . . . Burnett.' He had considerable difficulty
pronouncing the name. 'Seems to have blown his brains out
with a revolver.'

'When?'

'How the hell should I know? You're the inspector, not
me.'

'Then are you smart enough at least to have asked where
it happened?'

'Ca Na Torrina. His sister, Señorita Burnett, phoned the
post. She'd gone to his house because he hadn't answered
the phone and she found him dead.'

At the conclusion of the conversation, Alvarez returned
to the kitchen and sat. Dolores, who had been writing out
a shopping list with some difficulty—her schooling had
been very brief and she should have worn glasses—looked
up. 'Is it serious?'

'No. An Englishman has shot himself.'

'Mother of God! You call that not serious?'

'If a man shoots himself, there can't be the kind of

complications which upset a superior chief.' He spoke with grateful satisfaction.

He left the house ten minutes later. His new, blood-red Seat Ibiza was parked in front of the house and he stared at it with possessive admiration. Twenty years ago it would never have occurred to him that he could ever own a car; ten years ago, the limits of his ambitions had been a secondhand Seat 600; now, a magnificent new Ibiza was his. And since the age of miracles was therefore not past, why should he not eventually own the finca of his dreams with soil so rich that it grew tomatoes the size of pumpkins? He unlocked the driving door and smoothed out the seat cover before he sat.

The engine started immediately and he drove off. Eduardo was by the corner and he slowed down and waved; Eduardo acknowledged the wave, but nothing more. Too jealous to admit any admiration for the new car . . .

At the Lariax road he came to a halt at the Stop sign instead of going on regardless as he would have done in the 600. He began the drive along the narrow, twisting lane, bordered by stone walls, which passed through the centre of the Huerta de Llueso. Huerta meant market garden. Years ago, the land had grown all the fruit and vegetables that the villagers had needed. Now, both had to be imported because most of the properties were either owned by foreigners or let to them in the season and much of the land had been lost to swimming pools or to growing roses instead of radishes, plumbago instead of peppers, lawns instead of lettuces . . .

Ca Na Torrina was an old house without a garage or a drive, but on the opposite side of the road was a triangular-shaped piece of land, too small and awkward for profitable cultivation, and he parked the Ibiza there.

He stepped out of the car. Despite the many trees which surrounded him, part of the bay was distantly visible, as was Puig Antonia. Ignore the constant thudding of a pneumatic rock-breaker that was working nearby and listen only to the cicadas. Could anywhere in the world be fairer than this? The island had many names, but Fortunate Isle was the sweetest and perhaps the truest. Possibly the Garden of Eden had been here . . . He brought his thoughts down to earth and back to the present. On the far side of the road was a dead man who had killed himself; it had been no Eden for him.

He was half way across the lane when a man appeared around a corner and called to attract his attention. He stepped back into the shade of a holm oak and waited. His mother had said that the cicadas cried, 'Hurry. Hurry. Hurry.' But why they should have been so insistently frantic in a land of calm, he couldn't now remember.

The man, old, time-creased, dressed in a dirt-stained shirt and patched trousers, stepped off the road. He stared at Alvarez for several seconds, screwing up his eyes against the glare, then said: 'You're Dolores Ramez's cousin.'

'And you're García Goñi. D'you know anything about the English señor who's been shot?'

Goñi answered with scorn. 'Work the land, don't I? It was my old woman who heard the señorita scream, wasn't it, and who went to see what the trouble was and then called me.'

'The señorita is the dead man's sister?'

'So they say. Seems difficult to believe, them being so different.'

'How d'you mean?'

Goñi brushed his thick, calloused hand across his forehead as he considered the question and tried to find the words to express what he wanted to say; the sunlight picked out a deep scar on the right-hand side of his face, the stubble on his chin, and several pieces of chaff in his grey, curly hair. 'She'd always something to say,' he finally answered. 'Like with the goats a while back. I told her, they was hobbled and I'd put up a fence. Didn't do no good. She went on and on about what would happen if they broke free . . .' He stopped as a car rounded the corner a hundred metres above them and he watched this with the perpetual curiosity of a countryman until it had passed them and reached the corner below.

Alvarez moved forward and crossed the road and Goñi followed him into the overgrown garden and then continued speaking as if there'd been no interruption. '. . . and wouldn't listen to what I had to say. Knows everything, that one does.' There was more respect than resentment in his voice. 'One of the bloody goats had to break its hobbles and smash through the new fence and eat a geranium. You should have heard her! Said it was a very special geranium and the seed had cost a thousand pesetas and if my goats ate any more, I'd have to buy new seed. As if I'm such a bloody fool as to believe any flower seed could cost that sort of money.'

Alvarez watched a hoopoe fly in curves and dip out of sight behind some orange trees. 'And what of the brother?'

'Completely different. Never said anything. Didn't give orders like she does.'

'It was she who found him, wasn't it?'

'She'd come up to see him, like she often did. Shot himself. Bloody silly thing to do.'

'I imagine she was very upset?'

'She's a real tough 'un, but she was crying away just like a local.'

'She'll have been badly shocked. I don't suppose the señor's a pretty sight?'

'There's some blood on his head,' replied Goñi dismissively. During a long life, which had spanned action in the Civil War, he had seen far worse sights.

'Is the house open?'

'I don't know how she's left it, do I?'

'You weren't the last out?'

'How do I know?'

Alvarez's patience when dealing with the peasant mentality was almost inexhaustible. 'Anyway, as far as you can tell, it's not locked up?'

'That's right.'

'Then I'll see if I can get inside.'

'You'll not be wanting me any more?'

'Not right now.'

'Then I'll get back to work.'

Alvarez had turned and crossed half way to the wooden front door when he remembered to ask: 'Where's the señorita live?'

Goñi, who had reached the road, stopped. 'What's that?'

Alvarez spoke much louder.

'Ca'n Pario, of course,' replied Goñi, contemptuous of such ignorance. He continued on his way, his movements ponderously deliberate after a lifetime of working the land.

The front door was shut, but not locked. Alvarez stepped into the entrada and from there into the sitting-room. He was surprised by the rows of leather-bound books and wondered how any man could be clever enough to absorb such learning? Nothing else could have so clearly and immediately identified this as a house occupied by a foreigner.

He returned to the entrada and went from there into the sitting-room. Violent death always shocked him, not because the sight of injuries revolted him, although they did, but because it was so clear a statement that life was transitory. He approached the body.

Burnett had fallen sideways off a chair and lay slumped on the floor. The entrance wound was near enough in the centre of his forehead and looked surprisingly insignificant, since the flesh had largely closed, for a wound that had killed. Some blood had flowed on to the tiled floor and congealed. His face was white, his lips partially drawn back to reveal yellowing teeth. A metre away was a small, snub-nosed revolver which lay with muzzle pointing towards a butano fire in the corner of the room.

The dining-room table was circular, with a very thick top and a cumbersome central pillar; locally made, Alvarez thought. On it stood a three-parts-empty bottle of Bell's whisky, a used glass, and a typewriter. A sheet of paper had been wound into the typewriter and on this had been typed: 'I have to do this. But immortality can defeat death. *Si monumentum requiris, Paris, circumspice.*'

Alvarez scratched his right ear. The first sentence confirmed suicide, the second seemed to be meaningless since suicide seemed unlikely to make the Englishman immortal, and the third was so much Greek to him. He looked at the whisky. If the bottle had been full or near full to begin with, then perhaps there was the reason for the strange form of the suicide note.

He crossed to inspect the revolver. It had one of the shortest barrels he had ever seen and walnut chequered grips. Knowing that the grips could never record prints, he picked it up and then, using a handkerchief, broke it. There were five chambers and all were loaded; two of the bullets had been fired. He looked back at the body. There was only the one bullet wound visible. He put the revolver back on the floor, straightened up. A man could move after he had suffered a fatal wound that would normally be presumed to have occasioned instantaneous death and men who had been shot through the heart had been known to walk around before they collapsed and died. So had the señor suffered the mortal wound, yet after that involuntarily fired a second time before collapsing?

He carefully examined the floor and near the right-hand corner of the room found a lead bullet, so distorted that had he not known what he was looking for he might never have identified it. Close to the bullet were several chips of stone and some very fine powder and on the wall, not far from a framed photograph, there was a starred mark. Clearly, the bullet had pulverized the Mallorquin plaster and then crumpled against the stone underneath. A second, involuntary shot or—the thought occurred to him—a first one to make certain gun and ammunition were working? He picked up the bullet and dropped it into his right-hand trouser pocket, reminding himself as he did so that he ought at the first opportunity to find something more secure to put it into. Before turning away, he studied the photograph. It depicted a stone head, the top part of which had been cut off, that possessed a triangular nose but no other features. Modern art?

The telephone was in the entrada and he used it to speak to one of the local doctors, who carried out forensic work that did not require a specialist's knowledge, and to the mortician. Each said that he would be out immediately. Knowing that neither man would arrive for quite some time, Alvarez went out into the garden and moved a patio chair into the shade. Once seated, he closed his eyes, the better to appreciate the peace.

The doctor was a small, bustling man, an amateur archæologist who had for years been trying to interest his fellows in discovering and preserving the island's past. 'He died roughly between eight and twelve hours ago.'

'Can't you be a little more precise?' Alvarez asked.

'Not with the heat we've been suffering. In any case, you ought to know that at best it's always only a rough estimate.'

'Are there any other wounds?'

'Only bruising on his left shoulder which probably occurred when he fell off the chair.'

'It's all right to move the body now?'

'As far as I'm concerned. You said he lived here on his own, but his sister has a place nearby. Have you seen her?'

'Not yet. I thought it best to wait until I'd spoken to you.'

'It'll be a good idea to try to find out what sort of a state he was in over the last few days or weeks. I haven't had much experience in suicides, but I've never known one without a history of mental problems of some sort or another.'

'You're surely not saying you believe it might not be suicide?'

'Good God, no! Just suggesting you confirm things. The man was lucky, mark you, to hit himself in the brain, like that. It's all too easy to miss causing fatal damage and to end up alive but paralysed, a cabbage.'

One might be fit enough to run up Mount Everest, have just won the lottery, and be about to escort Miss Spain to dinner, thought Alvarez, but a quick chat with a doctor was enough to make one take to one's bed.

'Well, I've work for six so I'll be away.'

Alvarez said goodbye. He then spoke to the mortician who had arrived five minutes previously and gave orders for the body to be moved. That done, he checked the time. Did he speak to the señorita now or later? Later, he decided.

He locked up the house, crossed the lane to his car. He drove into the old square in the village, parked in a taxi rank, and went into the Club Llueso for a coffee and brandy.

Alvarez dialled Palma. The lady with a plum voice said: 'This is Superior Chief Salas's office.'

'It's Inspector Alvarez. When the superior chief returns, will you tell him . . .'

'Señor Salas has returned from Madrid. I'll put you through.'

'Hang on, there's no need . . .' He was ignored. He cursed himself for not having phoned before merienda, when he would have managed to miss his superior.

'Yes, what is it?' said Salas curtly.

'Señor, I have to report that an Englishman, Señor Burnett, committed suicide either late last night or early this morning by shooting himself in the head.'

'You are sure that he's dead?'

'Of course I am . . .'

'Don't you give me any "of course". When you report that a man is dead, I expect him to turn up very much alive within the week.'

'The doctor has examined his body.'

'Then provided he's considerably more competent than you, that should at least confirm that someone's dead. How d'you know he's Señor Burnett?'

'His sister identified him, as did a local farmer.'

'How d'you know it's suicide?'

'The evidence all supports that.'

'The evidence, or your interpretation of it?'

'There is a suicide note.'

There was a long pause. Finally, Salas said: 'Then it seems that for once I can accept a report of yours as accurate.'

CHAPTER 7

Alvarez stared up at the ceiling of his bedroom. There were, he thought, in every day two moments which epitomized pleasure and pain; when one closed one's eyes at the beginning of a siesta and when one opened them at the conclusion.

He sat upright and swivelled round on the bed until he could put his bare feet on the tiled floor. He looked at his watch. It was nearly five o'clock and he'd slept longer than he'd intended, but that surely meant that he'd needed the sleep even more than he'd realized?

He dressed in short-sleeved, open-neck shirt and cotton trousers, eased his feet into sandals. The window was wide open with the shutters shut, but even so the room was like an oven. Not the weather for rushing.

Downstairs, Isabel and Juan were watching television and Dolores was in the kitchen, beginning to prepare the supper. He slumped down on the stool. 'My God, it's so hot it's difficult to move!'

'Unless you're a woman who has to slave in a kitchen because her men can think only of their stomachs.'

These days, she was always complaining. Perhaps it was because of her age; there was a time of life when every woman became even more illogical than usual. Or perhaps it was the pernicious influence of all that nonsense about women needing their own identities. Jaime should long ago have taught her that it was a woman's privilege, not her penance, to look after her menfolk, but he was too scared of arousing her wrath . . .

'Well?' she demanded. 'You feel like telling me something?'

He hastily shook his head.

She turned back to the stove and stirred the diced onion, just beginning to hiss, in a saucepan. 'Aren't you working this afternoon?'

'Yes, of course. I've a lot to do.'

'Then why aren't you out, doing it?'

'I thought . . . I was hoping you would be very kind and make me some coffee before I leave.'

'Men! As polite as debtors when they want something!'

Twenty minutes later he drove to La Huerta and Ca'n Pario, which proved to be roughly half a kilometre down from Ca Na Torrina. He parked by the side of a large estanque set back from the lane, and walked up a rough dirt track to a small caseta, the kind of place in which the poorer peasants, farming on a share-cropping basis, had once lived.

He knocked on the front door of the single floor, drystone building, turned and looked out across the land. The garden was a profusion of plants and shrubs, at times inextricably mixed, many of which were in flower; the kind of garden of which he approved—that was, if land had to be wasted— since it was sufficiently haphazard in form to suit the setting.

Beyond was a large field in which, under regularly spaced orange, lemon, and loquat trees, were being grown beans, tomatoes, sweet peppers, aubergines, melons, and late potatoes.

The door opened and he turned back. The moment he saw the señorita, he remembered her. Some nine months previously he had been investigating the theft of a bicycle and in the course of those investigations had questioned a boy. The señorita had appeared and told him, in no uncertain manner, that he was an idiot if he thought that the boy could have anything to do with a missing bike since he was the son of a friend of hers. Overwhelmed by the vehemence of her illogical argument, he had accepted the boy's innocence, gratified to find a foreigner who concerned herself so sympathetically (if aggressively) with the islanders. His sense of gratitude had in no way been diminished when, later, he'd discovered that the boy had in fact taken the bike. 'Señorita,' he said in English, 'I am Inspector Alvarez of the Cuerpo General de Policia.'

She replied in Spanish. 'Please come in.'

To his initial surprise, she was not wearing black, but a cotton frock in quite bright colours. But any suggestion that such lack of mourning denoted lack of suffering was negated by the expression on her heavily featured face. He stepped into the house, noticeably cool because of the thick walls. 'Señorita, I am very distressed by what has happened. Please believe me that I would not be troubling you if it were not absolutely necessary.'

'It may be better to have someone to talk to,' she said wearily.

He wanted to ask if she did not have friends to whom she could turn in this time of grief, but knew that the question might well be resented. Foreigners, and especially the British, did not always wish to share their grief, unlike the Mallorquins.

The living-room had uneven stone walls which year after

year had been painted white with cal so that now this was over a centimetre thick, and a sloping roof with exposed timber beams. Small initially, it had been made smaller by the bookshelves and free-standing bookcases filled with a few hardcover, but mainly softcover books. Set in front of the open fireplace were two well worn chairs; the seat of one had on it a pile of books and she picked these up. 'You can sit here, now. Books are my one luxury.' She put the books down on the floor, sat on the second chair. 'My parents taught us . . .' She stopped, nibbled her upper lip above which there grew a vestigial moustache. 'They taught us to love books. I remember how, when every penny became important, I still would buy . . . But you haven't come to hear an old woman rambling on about the past.'

'Señorita, I have come to try and understand the tragedy and therefore I must learn as much as is possible.' If she talked at length, he thought, she might be able to ease a little of her sorrow.

'I imagine you drink?' she asked abruptly.

'Yes, señorita.'

'Would you be shocked if I offered you a drink this early in the evening?'

'Why should I be?'

'Of course you wouldn't. I'm not thinking straight. The Mallorquins are far too sensible ever to suffer the British hypocrisy of calling for the sun to be over the yardarm before drinks are served. You're a straightforward people and I'm sure that that's because until recently you've all been close to the things in life which really matter. Your tragedy is that in the past twenty years, you've been pitch-forked into the consumer society and now the young think that a new car is more important than a new plough.'

He further warmed towards a foreigner who recognized that there could be merit in simplicity and stupidity in sophistication.'

'I can offer you wine or coñac; which would you like?'

'Coñac, please, with perhaps a little ice?'

She stood, crossed to the doorway on the far side of the room and went through into the kitchen. Behind him was another doorway and that would give access to a single bedroom. Either off the bedroom or the kitchen would be a bathroom—so small it probably could not hold a bath, only a shower. That was the extent of the caseta. There was another link here with his early life. He had been born in a place no larger than this and he, his brother and his sister, had slept in the same room as their parents. They had learned much at an early age . . .

She returned and handed him a tumbler which was half filled with brandy in which floated three ice cubes. As soon as she was seated, he said: 'You were beginning to tell me how your parents had taught you to like books, señorita.'

She stared into the past; a shaft of sunshine, coming through the single, high-up window, provided a sharp back-cloth to her profile, emphasizing both strength and stubbornness. 'I was the elder and right from the beginning Mother used to read to me; later, of course, it was to both of us. She said that if one loved books one could be poor but travel the world, be a nobody who met the famous, be alone and yet surrounded by friends. I suppose I didn't understand the truth of that until Father lost all his money and we were left with little but books.' She drank. 'Justin could never gain as much pleasure from them as I did and I've always thought that that was because Father was old-fashioned enough to believe that reading should always improve one's mind and therefore to read solely for pleasure was not only a waste of time, but also rather sinful. So while I was left to read what I wanted, be it Jane Austen or Margery Allingham—I was only a woman, so Father didn't bother about the state of my education—Justin was instructed in what was permissible and what was not. He loved Henty and Ballantyne, but had to conceal the fact that he even knew the names . . . When he came here to live, he brought out Father's library, but I'm certain he never opened any of the books. He felt he had to honour his father's memory by maintaining the library, yet at the same time could now prove his independence by not reading a book from it. Without ever realizing it, parents weave tight nets for their children, and the more certain the parents are that what they're doing is right, the more dangerous and damaging the nets become.' She drained her glass. 'I've always been grateful that I've never had the impossibly difficult task of bringing up a child.'

He wondered how truthful she was being? The old were adept at suborning wishes to results. Why hadn't she married? When young, she must have been good company, even if no beauty. Intelligent men were as attracted by character as by looks. Had there been a romance which had ended in tragedy? As his had, when Juana-María had been pinned against the wall by a drunken French driver . . .

'Father was old-fashioned over more than books. He believed that stern discipline put backbone into a boy. Mother tried to make him understand that Justin needed to be treated sympathetically, but he wouldn't listen. For him, Justin's habits and ways of thought marked him as "soft" and a "soft" man was a weak one. Of course, all this made Justin very resentful. In fact, when we learned Father had lost his money, Justin was frightened, naturally, but he was also . . . well, just a little glad, despite the bleak future, because it showed that Father was far from the perfect man he seemed—to Justin, at least—to set himself up as . . .' She stopped, was silent for a moment, then said as she stood: 'You'll have another?'

'Thank you.' He handed her his glass.

She went through to the kitchen, returned, handed him back his glass, sat. 'You have to remember that Justin had a very uncertain younger life. If one's had security and this is suddenly snatched away so that one has to learn how harsh the world can be, one's bound to be bewildered and resentful.'

Security had vanished for her as well, he thought, but she had overcome the loss and, rather than being weakened by the experience, had been strengthened by it. 'Was he ever married?'

'Before my father died, more to get away from home than any other reason. She was a pleasant creature, but with a very limited and conventional mind. Always worrying about what other people thought.'

Which, surely, the señorita never did. 'Were they divorced?'

'No. She died after he retired.'

'Looked at broadly, would you say it was a successful marriage?'

'They were too far apart, emotionally and intellectually, for that. She couldn't take the slightest interest in his job and attacked him because his income was relatively low and wouldn't begin to understand that to him, far more important than money was the fact that he had a chance to prove himself a man of consequence.' There was pride in her voice as she continued: 'He'd always had a very strong interest in the arts and for quite a time he worked in eighteenth-century paintings. Then he made a complete switch—the only time he did anything so revolutionary— to the Greco-Roman periods. When he retired, he was curator of the Greek and Roman department of the Northern Museum and an acknowledged expert on some matters. Sotheby's sometimes consulted him. He wrote a book on Roman armour that one critic called definitive. Yet all his wife could do was complain that this book didn't sell tens of thousands of copies like the latest romantic mush did. She wanted to buy new curtains, because their neighbours had just hung new ones and his book didn't make enough money for that.'

'Did he come to live here soon after she died?'

'It was quite a while later. You see, he was not a man who normally would ever take a risk unless it seemed he

had to. After she died, he was obviously lonely and I wrote
and suggested he came out here because most people are
prepared to be so much more friendly; but he wouldn't.'

'He didn't have many friends?'

'The marriage had made certain of that. He liked intelligent people, she didn't, so while she was alive she made his
friends unwelcome and naturally they stopped visiting. After
she died, he didn't want to keep up with her friends and
since he was no longer meeting people at work, there was
no one left.'

'What changed his mind about coming here?'

'He had a very nasty car crash and was badly injured. I
went home to help after he left hospital and when I saw
how very depressed he'd become, I bullied him into selling
up and moving out.'

'Did he enjoy living here?'

'At first, yes, he did. Because we're a small expatriate
community, differences in backgrounds often don't seem to
matter so much. He saw a lot of people, some of whom
were of a similar intellectual background. But then the
after-effects of the crash began to trouble him and he with-
drew into himself and stopped seeing many of the
people . . .' She sighed. 'To be honest, he let the problems
overwhelm him rather than fight back.'

'What were these after-effects?'

'Mainly headaches of increasing frequency and intensity.
A couple of months ago he returned to England and saw
the specialist who'd operated on him, but that didn't help.'

'Señorita, when you so tragically discovered him, did you
notice the gun on the floor?'

'Yes,' she answered harshly.

'Did you recognize it?'

'Father had owned it. When he died, Justin kept it and
brought it out here. I said that this was ridiculous and to
get rid of it, no one needed that kind of thing out here, but
he wouldn't.'

A revolver, Alvarez thought, often offered a suggestion of strength to a man who knew himself to be weak. 'From all you've told me, señorita, your brother was neither a fit nor a happy man. Sadly, it cannot be too much of a surprise that he chose to kill himself.'

'Justin wasn't a fighter.' Her voice was strained. 'But our family was a religious one and he never lost his faith. He couldn't have committed suicide. He must have been murdered.'

CHAPTER 8

They stood in the dining-room of Ca Na Torrina. The body had gone, but nothing else was missing. Alvarez hoped that she did not realize the significance of the stains on the tiled floor. 'Señorita, pain can be so severe that it alters a person's character, especially . . . well, especially if that person is not of a very strong nature. Is it not possible that the headaches the señor had been suffering had become so frequent and so severe that he decided he must find a release from them, despite the abhorrence of suicide that his religious upbringing had instilled in him?'

'No,' she answered flatly. 'Perhaps you're forgetting that it's a Christian duty to suffer, if called upon to do so.'

Could one ever be quite certain about how another person under extreme pressure would behave? he wondered. 'There is a suicide note. Perhaps you did not notice it?'

'No, I didn't. I . . . When I saw him . . .'

'Señorita, there is absolutely no need to explain.' He crossed to the typewriter, unwound the sheet of paper, handed it to her. He waited until she'd read it, then said: 'That makes it clear that he intended to take his own life.'

'It does nothing of the sort. On the contrary, it makes it clear that he did not.'

'I don't understand.'

'Justin was always very precise with words and never wrote in a mandarin style; if he'd written a suicide note, it would have been precise and immediately understandable. This was written by someone who thought that, being an academic by nature, Justin would have written it in what the writer regarded as an academic style.'

'You don't think that under such severe mental confusion, he might not have acted as he normally would?'

'This was written by someone else. It doesn't even make sense.'

'Do you understand the last sentence?'

She looked down at the paper again. 'If I remember correctly, it's the epitaph inscribed on Sir Christopher Wren's tomb in St Paul's Cathedral. It means: If you seek his monument, look around you. But in the original, of course, there is no mention of Paris.'

'Did your brother visit Paris very often?'

'Never, as far as I know. His wife would never have allowed him to go to a city of sin. She thought in clichés, most of them completely outdated.'

'Then why should there be this mention of Paris?'

'For the simple reason that it's nonsense. Traditionally, suicides are not of sound mind. So whoever typed out the bogus note tried to give the impression of a man of learning whose mind was unsound.'

He took the paper back from her, but instead of placing it on the typewriter, he folded it up and put it in his pocket.

'You don't believe me, do you?' she demanded.

'Señorita, I am certain that you are saying exactly what you believe to be true. But at such a time of great emotional stress . . .'

'I've been terribly shocked, but I'm not a hysterical female who can't face facts. Justin would never have committed

suicide. Even if he had, he would have explained why
sensibly, instead of writing nonsense in a ridiculous style.
But if you won't accept what I've told you, answer this:
Why is there a bottle of whisky on the table?'

'Forgive me, but all you have told me suggests that your
brother was not a man of natural courage and perhaps he
needed to drink to try to find some.'

'He never drank whisky.'

'Are you certain?'

She answered sharply: 'Of course I am. He actively
disliked it. He drank brandy, gin, and vodka, but never
whisky. He only kept it in the house for guests.'

'Perhaps there was no brandy, gin, or vodka available,
nevertheless he had to have a drink?'

She walked over to the far end of the dining-room and
to a large Mallorquin sideboard, extensively carved in a
traditional pattern. She opened the right-hand door, motioned with her hand.

He moved forward until he could see inside. He counted
three bottles of brandy, one opened, two of gin, one opened,
and two of vodka, both unopened. He said, his voice
troubled: 'Perhaps he did not realize, because of the state
of his mind, that he had taken out a bottle of whisky rather
than coñac . . .'

'Fiddlesticks!'

'Señorita, if one approaches all the questions you've raised
from a different viewpoint, then . . .'

'Approach them from this one. Who was it who'd been
arguing so violently with him in the morning?'

'How do you know someone had?'

'I walked up here to see him and heard the argument
going on. The other man was so heated, I was a little scared,
but I didn't do anything because Justin always became so
annoyed if he thought I was trying to . . . well, to support
him.'

The weak man, needing assistance but resenting any offer

of it because not only did that underline his own weakness, it also identified the other person's awareness of it. 'Did you recognize the voice?'

'No.'

'Have you any idea what the argument was about?'

'None whatsoever. I didn't stay in case Justin saw me.'

'At what time was this?'

'Around eleven.'

He rubbed his chin, which reminded him that he'd forgotten to shave that morning. 'Did you return and see your brother later on?'

'No. I phoned to make certain he was all right.'

'And was he?'

'So he said.'

'Did you ask him what had been the trouble?'

'No. Don't you see, I didn't want to seem to be prying and he'd have brought up the subject if he'd wanted me to know.'

'Were you able to make any judgement on his state of mind? Was he very depressed?'

'He sounded more cheerful than for a long time.'

'Señorita, what I must do now is to think about what you've just told me and then make the further investigations which will be necessary.'

'Remember the most important thing of all. Because of his beliefs, he could not have committed suicide.'

'I will not forget . . . If I discover that you are right, can you suggest what motive there might be for your brother's murder?'

'No.'

'He was not a rich man?'

'Far from it.'

'Has he recently been very friendly with a lady?'

'No. There really is nothing more I can tell you.'

'Then you will want to leave. It has been very kind of you to help.'

They left the sitting-room, crossed the entrance and went outside. The late sunshine highlighted the lines of sorrow in her face and he would have liked to comfort her, but found he lacked the words. In any case, he decided, she was of so independent a character that perhaps she would resent, rather than find comfort from, the solace of a foreign stranger.

When he returned to the dining-room, he stared at the bottle of whisky. How far did he accept her contention that no matter how desperate the turmoil in Burnett's mind, he would never have drunk whisky? . . . Whisky was such a universally liked drink that nothing would seem more natural to a murderer trying to suggest suicide after a bout of heavy drinking than to put a bottle on the table, little knowing that the dead man was one of the few who disliked it . . . He walked round the table and examined the wall, near the framed photograph of the blindly ugly stone head, where the bullet had struck. Nothing to say whether this had been fired to test that gun and ammunition were in working order, or a shot fired involuntarily during a struggle to gain possession of the revolver . . .

He shook his head. This had to be suicide and the señorita's wild assertions were those of a sister who could not, would not, accept that her brother had been as much a weakling at his death as during his life.

He left the house, locked the front door and pocketed the key. As he walked towards the small wooden gate, he heard a man singing, the song filled with the wailing intonations which dated it back to the time of the Moors. He turned away from the gate and pushed through the overgrown garden to the boundary fence. In the field beyond, Goñi was irrigating several rows of tomatoes.

He climbed over the fence and walked up between rows of beans and sweet peppers to where Goñi was working. 'Have you got a moment?'

Goñi might not have heard. He stared down at the rushing

water in the main channel, fed from a large estanque in one corner of the field, mattock held ready; when one side channel was filled, he stopped that off with the plug of earth taken from the next one, which now rapidly began to fill.

'Were you working here yesterday morning?'

Goñi looked up very briefly, his weatherbeaten face expressing contempt. 'D'you think I was down in the port, boozing my legs silly?'

'You've other fields; you might have been in one of them.'

'Well, I weren't.' He diverted the water to a fresh channel.

'Then did you hear anything unusual?'

'What d'you mean?'

Alvarez accepted that Goñi wasn't necessarily being bloody-minded; like most peasants, his life was lived in literal terms and therefore he liked things to be spelled out exactly, leaving no room for ambiguity.

Goñi opened up the last channel which fed tomatoes, hurried back along the main channel to the estanque where he turned off the large gate valve, cutting the rush of water. He stood on a rock to peer into the estanque.

'How's the water holding out for you?'

'There ain't enough,' he answered automatically. The estanque was fed by the aqueduct that came down from a spring in the Festna valley which, despite the growing shortage of water on the island, still flowed freely; but only a fool risked the gods' jeering wrath by boasting all was well.

Alvarez brought out a pack of cigarettes from his pocket. 'Smoke?'

'Giving something away! What are you after?'

'Information about yesterday morning.'

The sun dropped behind a mountain crest and abruptly they were in shadow; directly overhead, the sky became shaded with the mauve tinge that was seen only in midsummer; small birds began to sing, active once more now that the intense heat was easing. Alvarez struck a match and they lit their cigarettes. As frequently happened, the light breeze of earlier had died right away and the air was so calm that the smoke rose vertically for quite a while before lazily beginning to shred.

Alvarez leaned against the side of the estanque. 'When did you have your merienda yesterday morning?'

'Same time as always.'

'Which is when?'

'When I want it.'

'Do you reckon you wanted it before eleven?'

Goñi thought, finally decided he could admit as much. 'Aye.'

'When you were back at work, did you hear anything unusual from that direction?' Alvarez jerked his thumb in the direction of Ca Na Torrina, hidden from them by the estanque.

Goñi hawked, spat. He smoked. Finally, he said: 'There was shouting. Is that what you're on about?'

'Who was shouting?'

'How should I know?'

'If it was the señor, you'd surely know?'

'Well, it wasn't.'

'Then who was it?'

'Ain't I just said? I don't know.'

'How many people were at it?'

'I only heard the one.'

'What kind of shouting was it?'

'Bloody loud.'

'D'you think it was an argument?'

'It wasn't someone being friendly, that's for sure.'

'This man was angry?'

'Sounded like he was bloody crazy.'

'What language was he shouting in?'

'Wasn't Mallorquin or Spanish.'

'English?'

After a while, Goñi said it might have been English.

'How long did the argument go on for?'

A shrug of the shoulders.

'Was it a long or a short time?'

'Time enough for me to go off and harness up the old mule and be back and him to be at it still.'

'Did you catch sight of whoever was doing the arguing?'

'Too busy working.'

'Is there anything about him you can tell me?'

'Only that he'd a bloody big red Mercedes that was in the sitjola.'

'The what?'

'The bit of land opposite the house that's not good for anything, of course.'

'Of course. How can you be certain it was his car?'

'Who else is going to park there?'

Alvarez drew on the cigarette a last time, dropped the butt to the ground and carefully ground it into the dust with the heel of his shoe. 'Did you see the señor after all this?'

'Saw him not long after the car drove off.'

'How did he seem?'

'Looked like . . .' Goñi scratched his head.

'Like he was really upset?'

'Like he was kind of . . . Well, something good had happened.'

It was difficult to decide what Goñi really meant. A man who had just had a very bitter row and who, within roughly thirteen hours, was going to commit suicide, was hardly likely to be in a laughing mood. No, the expression had been false or Goñi had falsely interpreted it. 'This Mercedes you saw in the sitjola—have you any idea who it belongs to?'

'Never seen it before.'

'You say it was big and red—anything more you can tell me about it?'

'Only that it had dark windows.'

How accurate was the marque identification? Goñi, like most men of his generation, had never owned or driven a car and it might be supposed that he'd have very little interest in them and therefore would be unlikely to be able accurately to identify a make. But of all the consumer goods which had corrupted values, television and cars were the two which were the most popular and they had aroused the sharp interest of even the oldest and most reactionary of peasants.

Goñi looked up at the sky. 'I'd best be moving.'

'Just wait a second. Did you see the señorita yesterday morning?'

'Aye. When she had something to say about a wall at the end of her garden. By God, she's a tough 'un!' He spoke admiringly.

'Was this before you heard the row in Ca Na Torrina?'

'While it was going on. She walks up the road, listens for a moment, turns back.'

'I'd like to know who was around late last night, but I don't expect you were?'

'I was in bed and asleep, where anyone with any bloody sense was.' He stomped off, then came to a stop just before he reached a turn in the dirt track. 'Oi!'

'Yes?'

'I've just remembered. The Mercedes was on tourist plates.' He continued on his way.

If the bitter row had had anything to do with Burnett's death, it probably was that it had further depressed him and edged him that much closer to committing suicide (the expression Goñi had noted might well, in fact, have been one of exhausted relief; the final decision had been made). But because the señorita was a woman of such determination, she was going to say that it had led up to her brother's death, almost certainly at the hands of the unknown man who had had that blazing row. Alvarez sighed. It seemed there was no longer any option left to him. Very soon, he was going to have to report to Salas.

CHAPTER 9

Alvarez replaced the receiver, slumped back in the chair and stared at the top of his desk without seeing the jumble of papers, files, memoranda, and letters that lay strewn all over it. He had spoken to an assistant at the Institute of Forensic Anatomy and asked him to check specifically whether the wound in Burnett's head had been self-inflicted and whether on his hand there were powder residues to prove he had fired a gun. He had also spoken to the fingerprint department and asked them to check the revolver for prints and had accepted, without voicing any resentment, the jeering comment that because of the shape of any revolver, it seldom recorded a print of consequence, and that one with a chequered handgrip was even less likely to do so. Soon, he would go back to Ca Na Torrina, put a fresh piece of paper in the typewriter, and type out the suicide note in order to confirm, by a comparison test, that the original had been typed on the machine on the dining-room table . . . All work carried out because when he telephoned his superior chief and informed him of the latest development, Salas would, in his normal discourteous and aggressive manner, demand to know if the investigations were being carried out efficiently.

He looked up and through the opened window which, since the sun was not yet on it, he had left unshuttered. Before he rang Salas, it would undoubtedly be an idea to slip out to the club and have a coffee and a brandy; after all, any sensible bullfighter prayed long and earnestly before he went into the ring.

He stood, crossed to the door, then came to a sudden stop as he realized that he had not yet phoned Traffic and asked them to identify all red Mercedes on tourist plates. If he'd spoken to Salas before doing that . . .

Alvarez said: 'Señor, there can be no doubt. But when the señorita made this claim, I decided I had to undertake a full investigation.'

'In other words, unbelievably you've managed to complicate even a simple suicide!'

'Not I, the señorita. As you so rightly say, señor, it is a simple suicide. But the señorita is English . . .'

'This has nothing to do with nationalities; it has everything to do with your inability to deal with any matter in a sane and sensible manner. Had you been in charge of the case, we still wouldn't know who murdered Abel.'

'But when the señorita said . . .'

'Elderly foreign señoritas say and do the most ridiculous things; I expect my inspectors to recognize that fact. Which, of course, is a mistake since it is necessary to remember that among my inspectors is one who is incapable of distinguishing between what is and what is not ridiculous.'

'Do you wish me to close the case?'

'How in the devil can you do that when you've allowed her to make this ridiculous allegation?'

'Where the señorita's concerned, it's more a case of what she . . .'

'I doubt it's even crossed your mind to ask for a test for powder residues?'

'I have arranged that.'

'What about the gun?'

'That is with the prints department.'

'And the typewritten suicide note?'

'That, together with a comparison note typed on the machine in question, is being forwarded to the laboratory.'

'And the car?'

'Traffic have been asked to prepare a list of all red Mercedes on tourist plates.'

'The bottle of whisky and glass?'

Alvarez silently swore. How could he have forgotten them?

Salas allowed the silence to continue for some time, then said: 'Even allowing for so many unfortunate occurrences in the past, I am still surprised that you could fail to see the need to have both bottle and glass tested for prints.'

'Señor, I was intending . . .'

'Your convoluted road to hell must be luxuriously paved with good intentions . . . Should there be prints on either, these will need to be compared with the dead man's prints.'

'Naturally, I will see . . .'

'And should there be some which are not the dead man's, perhaps it will be best if you get in touch with me so that I can try to explain the full significance of this.'

'I do understand . . .'

'An assumption I would prefer never to make.'

Alvarez parked in the sitjola for the second time that morning, crossed the road, unlocked the front door of Ca Na Torrina and went inside. There was a flash of movement on the right-hand wall of the entrada as a gecko made a lunge for, and caught, a small moth. Then it 'froze', no doubt hoping that it would be ignored by the intruder.

He went through to the dining-room and packed the bottle of whisky and glass in cardboard containers, using bubbled plastic to make certain that they were held tightly in place. Burnett's prints would be on both, he assured himself as he left. Stress could alter a person's behaviour out of all recognition; it might easily have left Burnett quite unaware of what he was drinking.

He followed a large Volvo shooting-brake down the narrow, twisting lane, then drew off into the parking space in front of the estanque by Ca'n Pario. As he opened the gate and stepped through, it occurred to him that the difference between this garden and that of Ca Na Torrina was not a bad indication of the difference between the characters of sister and brother.

Phillipa, wearing a shapeless hat with a wide, floppy brim, a brightly coloured frock, and flip-flops, was sitting in the shade of a tree. She had been reading and as he approached she carefully inserted a leather marker, closed the book.

'Señorita, I hope I do not disturb you?'

'I'm always glad of company. Do sit down.' She waited until he was seated, then said: 'As a matter of fact, I was going to telephone you. I want to know when I can go ahead and arrange the funeral.'

He said, very sympathetically: 'Señorita, I am very much afraid that for the moment it is impossible to answer you. Certain inquiries have to be concluded.'

'You mean, there has to be a post-mortem?'

He might have known that she would want to face the facts. 'Yes, señorita.'

'Then you now believe that Justin did not commit suicide?'

'The post-mortem is required because of the nature of his death, whatever the possible cause.'

She fidgeted with the cover of the paperback. 'The cause is, he was murdered.'

'The facts have yet to be established and I have asked for certain tests to be conducted. Nothing more can be said until the results of these are known.'

'You sound as if you still think it was suicide?'

'I'm afraid I do.'

'That is quite impossible.'

He decided it was no good arguing. She would remain convinced that her brother's death had not been suicide because she was so loath to face the truth of his ultimate weakness until it finally became impossible to do so.

'I presume you're here because there's something more you want to know?'

'Yes, señorita.'

'Well, before I tell you anything, I need a drink and I don't suppose you'll refuse one. Will you have coñac?'

'Thank you very much.'

He watched her stand, go into the house. Indomitable was the word which occurred to him. Naturally still deeply shocked, yet determined not to show such 'weakness'. The famed stiff upper lip. But would she not have found it easier to come to terms with events had she been able to give way to her grief?

She returned, handed him a tumbler that was three parts full of brandy and ice, sat. 'What do you want to know now?'

'When you walked up to your brother's house on Monday morning, did you happen to notice if there was a car parked in the sitjola opposite?'

'There was one, yes.'

'Did you recognize it?'

'No, I didn't go far enough up the road to see more than the top half of it above the stone wall.'

'Have you the slightest idea what was the subject of the violent row?'

'As I think I said before, none whatsoever.'

'Your brother hadn't mentioned to you anything which had happened or had been said by or to him which conceivably could have led to so fierce an argument?'

'In the past few months he's seen hardly anyone except a couple of close friends and it's impossible it could have been anything to do with either of them.'

'Do you know of anyone who actively disliked him?'

'An expatriate community like this one always has its quota of backbiting scandal-mongers and suddenly disintegrating friendships. But Justin . . . Well, he was the kind of person who didn't arouse sharp emotions in other people.'

Yet it seemed he had aroused a very violent rage in someone. 'You told me he wasn't wealthy, but would you say he was comfortably off?'

'That all depends on your terms of reference, doesn't it? Compared to some of the people out here, he was a pauper; compared to me, he was comfortably off.'

'Would you know what happens to his estate?'

'I have a copy of his will, he had a copy of mine. I am his sole beneficiary.'

'Do you have a rough idea of how much his estate will amount to?'

'By today's standards, very little. When he lived in England, his only capital was his house, his only income the museum pension and the old age pension. He decided, wisely, not to use the money he gained from selling his house to buy another one out here, but to buy himself an annuity which would greatly increase his income. He spoke to a broker and asked what would be the best kind of annuity which would . . .' She became silent.

He waited patiently.

'Even though I often bullied him for his own good, he was always very fond of me. He knew how hard up I was because of the frightening rise in the cost of living out here, and that while he could help me financially—as he did— while he was alive, if he died before I did and all his capital had been invested in an annuity, he'd not be able to leave me anything. So he told the broker that as well as the annuity, he wanted to take out some form of life insurance that would ensure that if he died within ten years—which he reckoned would see me out; I hope he was right—I would benefit by inheriting a capital sum. Because of his age, the insurance was very expensive, but he didn't mind because he was making as certain as he could that I'd be all right.'

'Did he tell you how much the insurance was for?'

'Twenty thousand pounds. I suppose that gives me a motive?'

'A motive?' he repeated, his mind not on his words.

'For having killed him.'

He was startled. 'Señorita! Not for one second could such a possibility be considered.'

'It's not unknown for siblings to murder.'

'Had you committed so unthinkable an act, would you have insisted—as you have done right from the beginning —that it had to be murder and not suicide? Would you not have done everything possible to make me believe that it was suicide? No, señorita, if your brother was murdered, the one person who could not be the murderer would be you.'

The first telephone call was at ten-fifteen the following morning.

'The deceased died as a result of a single shot fired when the muzzle of the gun was within one centimetre of the temple. The skin surrounding the entrance hole was burned the typical grey-brown colour and there was the expected smeary coat of powder residue. The bullet remained embedded in the back of the skull.

'The site of the wound is such that it could have been either self-inflicted or occasioned by another party.

'The deceased's hands have been tested for powder tattooing. There are traces on both hands.'

'What's that?'

'Both.' There was a pause and then the speaker said, his tone now ironic: 'So what do you make of that?'

Alvarez was about to say that it was impossible when he remembered that two shots had been fired. Even so . . .

'There are areas of bruising on the shoulder, but these are consistent with his having fallen from a chair to the ground. He was in reasonably good physical condition, having regard to his age, except for a past injury to his skull.

'He had ingested a considerable amount of alcohol shortly before his death and the concentration in his blood was around point two per cent. That means he was past the delightful stage, but not yet at the dead drunk one.'

'Can you distinguish whether it was grape or grain alcohol?'

'That problem's with the lab boys and you'll have to get the answer from them.'

Alvarez thanked him, rang off, drummed on the desk with his fingers. He checked in the telephone directory for Phillipa's number, dialled it. 'Señorita, I must apologize for bothering you yet again, but I need to know something. Was your brother right or left-handed?'

'Left-handed. Father tried to make him change, but only succeeded in making him stutter.'

'Could he use his right hand more easily than a right-handed man can usually use his left?'

'He was never able to write right-handed, but there were other things he trained himself to do right-handed because that was easier. Why do you ask?'

'There is something which has to be answered and it matters which hand he favoured.'

When the call was over, he slumped back in the chair. If it had been suicide, then Burnett must have wanted to make certain he did not mistake his aim and would have fired the fatal shot with his left hand. So was it even remotely feasible to imagine that he'd have fired the first, and exploratory, shot at the wall with his right hand? Against his will, Alvarez began to envisage a scene. The man with whom Burnett had had such a bitter row in the morning had returned that night, his anger increased rather than abated. Burnett, frightened, had sought to defend himself with the revolver. There had been a struggle, the intruder had managed to get hold of the gun and had shot Burnett. He had then set out to hide his murder under the guise of suicide. Knowing that when one fired a gun one was normally left with a powder tattoo, he had put the gun in the dead man's hand and manipulated it so that a second shot, aimed at the wall, was fired . . . Never stopping to remember what previous observation should have told him: Burnett was left-handed.

CHAPTER 10

Traffic rang at a quarter to one. 'About your inquiry re red Mercedes on tourist plates. There are seventy-five on the island.'

'Hell! It'll take days to check up on that many,' said Alvarez gloomily.

'Have you any further details that might help to cut down the numbers?'

'Only that the man who saw it made a point of how big it was.'

'Then it could be one of the larger models rather than a 190. Let me check what difference that would make.' There was a long pause. 'That would leave sixteen cars, ranging up to a 560 which by all accounts is big enough for an oil sheik and his four wives.'

'Give me the names and addresses of the sixteen owners, will you?'

When the call was over, Alvarez stared down at the list. It seemed reasonable to suppose the car was owned by someone who lived close to Llueso, simply because most car journeys were short ones. Yet against that, the señorita had not recognized the man's voice and since she probably knew everyone locally who was rich enough to have such a car, this suggested a stranger from another part of the island. What could have brought a stranger to argue so bitterly with a man who had virtually become a recluse? Again, what motive for murder could a stranger have?

It was, he thought sadly, a familiar experience. After much laborious work, both mental and physical, he propounded a sequence of events which logically fitted the facts—only to discover subsequently that logically such a sequence could not have occurred. Chasing around the circumference of a circle to discover where it began . . .

Some two kilometres beyond Santa Lucía, Alvarez turned off the tarmac on to a dirt track. As the car bounced on the rough surface, he slowed right down, cursing because a man could not hope to keep his car in pristine condition when travelling so rough a surface. A notice with the name Ca'n Heal, shaped as an arrow, pointed off to the right. Happily, this new track was metalled and he no longer strained his ears to hear a spring snapping, a shock-absorber falling off, or the sump's being ruptured. The track passed through a belt of trees, mostly pine, then straightened to line up on a house. He whistled. This foreigner had bought a piece of Mallorquin history. Not even in his wildest daydreams had he ever imagined himself living in such a mansion; when he'd been young only the aristocracy had owned such properties and even if a frog could turn into a prince, a peasant could never become an aristocrat.

He parked, climbed out of the car. The garden was a banked mass of colour, overwhelming in its extravagance; many of the flowers were familiar, but others he had never seen before; several of the flowering trees were covered in such a profusion of blossom that they looked theatrically unreal; the large lawn, a deep green, had been newly mown. He wondered how much water was needed to keep all these plants, trees, and lawn, alive and flourishing in the height of the summer and could only come up with the answer that it was a prodigal waste of resources that took one's breath away.

He crossed to the wooden front door, panelled in one of the traditional Mallorquin square patterns. Age had cracked yet toughened the wood, repeated applications of gas oil had darkened it, and the sun had baked it. For centuries, that door had closed off the harsh outside world from the few inside who believed the luxury of a pleasant, refined life to be no more than a right . . .

The door was opened by a young woman, wearing a white apron over a blue frock, whose manner was as pert as the expression in her eyes. 'Is Señor Heal in?' he asked.

'No, he's not.' She showed him no respect, having judged him by his appearance.

'When do you expect him back?'

'What's that to you?'

'Cuerpo General de Policía.'

She was not now frightened, as anyone might have been twenty years before, but she had become wary. 'Well, I'm sorry, but I just don't know when he'll return, except it'll likely be before eight since he told Carolina he'd be eating here tonight.'

'Is Señora Heal in?'

'There's no señora; leastways, not one that lives here. Not yet.' She giggled.

'Is there any other family?'

'The señorita, his daughter, was here earlier, wanting to talk to him; I don't rightly know whether she's still around.'

'Perhaps you'd find out? I'd like a word with her if she is here.'

'You'd best come in, then.'

He was shown into a very large room; once the ballroom? he wondered, uncertain whether a manor house would have had one. It was filled with furniture, hangings, carpets, display cabinets, and paintings, all of which to his uneducated eye looked valuable. It was, he decided, a room to make a man very careful not to belch aloud.

The far door opened and a young woman entered. 'Good afternoon. I understand you are . . .' She searched for the word in Spanish.

'Inspector Alvarez, señorita,' he replied in English. He preferred women to be dressed smartly, but had to admit to himself that she lost nothing through wearing a loose-fitting linen shirt and faded jeans. Perhaps that was because she was beautiful in a way that owed nothing to glamour and everything to character. Both the maid's attractions and hers were obvious, but the maid's raised images of lust while hers called forth only honourable thoughts . . .

'Is there some way in which I can help you, even though Father's out?'

He jerked his mind down from the heady heights of knightly chivalry. 'I would like to ask the señor a few questions concerning his car, but the maid said he's out. Perhaps you could answer them?'

'I doubt it. I don't live here and I only came along to . . . Well, like you, I wanted a word and didn't know he was out.'

There was, briefly, a note of bitterness in her voice. An unhappy relationship between father and daughter? 'Señorita, it may be possible that nevertheless you can help me. The señor owns a red Mercedes on tourist plates. Does it have darkened glass?'

She frowned slightly. 'Why d'you want to know?'

'I need to identify the owner of one such Mercedes because he may be able to help me.'

'Help you in what way?'

'With an inquiry I am conducting.'

'I can tell you for certain that Gerry's not been involved in any road accident.'

'There is no suggestion of that.'

'Then why . . .' She did not finish the question. After a moment, she said: 'I can't see that it's a state secret. Yes, his Merc does have tinted glass.'

'Since he lives reasonably close to Llueso, I imagine he drives there or to the port quite frequently?'

'That sounds reasonable.'

'And he'll know a number of other foreigners who live there?'

'Look, you'd better be a bit more specific about why you're asking these questions.'

'There has been an unfortunate incident in Llueso. Señor

Burnett has died in unusual circumstances. Now, it is necessary for me to find out exactly what happened and the
owner of a large red Mercedes on tourist plates, with tinted
windows, may be able to help me. If it was the señor's car
in Llueso on Monday morning, he almost certainly will be
able to.'

'I can give you the answer now, it won't be his. He was
here all morning.'

'I see . . . Still, it'll be best if I just ask him to confirm
that. I will return here tomorrow morning at about eleven.
But if that's not convenient, will you ask him to telephone
me to say what time will suit him?'

She nodded.

'Perhaps you could give me some paper and a pencil so
that I can write down the telephone number?'

She walked over to the nearer door. She moved with the
unconscious grace of a fawn; beneath those casual clothes
there must be slender limbs of ivory . . . He cursed himself
for such crude, sensual thoughts. Put a swine in a castle, he
still had swinish thoughts.

When she returned, she handed him a small pad and a
ballpoint pen. He wrote down the telephone number of the
post and his name, handed back pad and pen.

'I still don't understand . . .' She tailed off into silence.
'All right, I'll tell him or else leave a message.'

He said goodbye and left, making his way back into the
huge entrance hall and out to his car.

CHAPTER 11

Alvarez parked in front of Ca'n Heal and climbed out into
the burning sunshine. In a bed beyond the lawn, a man was
tying tall-stemmed flowers to bamboo stakes. Even in the
heyday of the aristocrats, he thought, no labourer had ever

been employed solely to grow and tend unproductive things; they might have lived in luxury while all those about them were in abject poverty, but they'd never lacked a sense of values.

He crossed to the front door and rang the bell. A middle-aged woman opened the door and he introduced himself.

'I'm sorry, but the señor's not here,' she said. 'He had a telephone call and had to go out suddenly. He said he'll be back as soon as possible and would you mind waiting?'

It was far more pleasant here than in his stuffy office. She showed him into a much smaller room than he had been in the previous day, furnished in a less overpowering manner.

'Would you like a coffee; or something stronger?' She was dumpy and wore glasses that gave her an owl-like appearance; but she had a quick and ready smile. She spoke Mallorquin with the harsher accent of the west coast.

'I'd not say no to a coñac.'

She brought him a brandy and when it became clear he would like to talk, she settled in one of the brocade-covered armchairs and accepted a cigarette.

She smoked in a nervous manner, constantly scraping the ash away into an ashtray, as if it were something she did not do very often. 'The señor's all right to work for, just so long as you do exactly what he wants. I said to Frederico, maybe you are right and he's wrong, but don't go on arguing, just do it his way. It's the man who owns the mule who says when it works. But he went on arguing. I've never met a man so stubborn.'

'Who's Frederico?'

'He worked in the garden along with Rafael until Thursday, when he was sacked. I said, the señor's a man who knows exactly what he wants and he's paying to get it. If you can't understand that . . . Frederico couldn't.'

'I met the señor's daughter yesterday.'

'She's nice. Mind you, if she wants something, she can be just as tough as him. But normally she's friendly and has a bit of a chat, which he never does. Wants to keep his distance from the likes of us.'

'What makes you say she can be hard at times?'

'As to that, you've only got to see the look that's sometimes in her eyes or the way she holds her chin. Or are you like my Fernando who only ever sees one thing in any woman?' She chuckled. 'But if you'd any doubts, you ought to have heard 'em last night, having a tremendous row. I thought to myself: For once, señor, you're getting as good as you give.'

'What was it all about?'

'Can't say, not speaking much English and in any case, I only heard 'em from the kitchen when I went there to get something. You see, I wasn't cooking a meal because the señor was on his own and sometimes when that happens he says he'll just have something cold and I leave it ready for him.'

'But you said he wasn't on his own, his daughter was there.'

She shrugged her shoulders. 'I suppose the señorita turned up unexpectedly. I mean, if he'd known she was coming to dinner, he'd certainly have asked for something cooked and Fernando in his white coat and gloves, serving. Even when it's his own daughter, the señor wants things done in the grand manner.'

'You're quite certain it was her.'

'I heard her, didn't I?'

'You said, not very clearly.'

'Fernando saw her car outside.'

'Then there's no doubt . . . Where's she living now?'

'Used to be in France, with her mother, and she visited here from time to time, but recently she's been on the island, living with a painter over at Costanyi. Maybe that's what they were arguing about. The señor's had more women here than I could count easily, but he doesn't like his daughter acting the same way.'

Her words shocked Alvarez. He had seen Alma in a
virginal light and to discover she was living with some
painter . . . It was, of course, the destruction of perfection
he found so painful, not the fact that she had a boyfriend . . .

'The painter's been here a couple of times; trying to sell
his paintings to the señor, like as not.'

He tried to speak normally, but was conscious that his
voice had roughened slightly. 'Is he one of the long-haired
louts who call themselves artists to avoid working?'

'I wouldn't know about that.'

'From the way the maid spoke when I was last here, it
seems the señor's getting married soon?'

'That's right enough what the lady thinks! Looking at
her makes me wonder if he really knows what he's letting
himself in for.'

'How d'you mean?'

'She's eyes in the back of her head and says exactly what
she wants. If he thinks he'll fool her while he carries on with
other women, he's got a surprise coming!'

'If that's his idea, why get married?'

'Who knows why anyone marries anyone?' She chuckled.
'When I look at Fernando now, I can't remember why!'

He smiled, although her words made him sadder than
before. Perhaps the attraction of maturity was nothing but
a fallacy, perpetuated by mature men. 'I suppose the señor
entertains a lot?'

'That he does and it's only the best gets served. Like the
last dinner, when it was lobster to start with. Imagine what
that cost!'

'Not unless you give me a calculator . . . Tell me, have
you seen an English señor here called Justin Burnett?'

She thought for a moment, shook her head.

'Have you ever taken a telephone call from him?'

'I can't remember doing so. Of course, most times it's
Fernando or Carmen, the maid, who answer the phone
because I'm busy with the cooking.'

'Would you do me a favour? Go and ask your husband and Carmen whether Señor Burnett ever phoned here.'

She looked curiously at him, then stood, stubbed out her cigarette, left.

He finished the brandy and carefully placed the glass down on the coaster so that it did not mark the highly polished occasional table. If he were living in this house, he'd furnish it very much more simply . . . Fool! he told himself scornfully. If he were living in this house, it would only be as one of the servants.

She returned. 'Neither of 'em's ever heard the name. Comes from round here, does he?'

'From Llueso.'

'Then the señor'll probably know him, since he goes there regularly.'

'Was he there Monday morning?'

'Must have been. Always goes then to get the Sunday paper.'

He looked at his watch. 'Won't be long to lunch.'

'I can't think where the señor's got to. He said he'd be back just as soon as he could be.'

'I'll hang on just a little longer.'

'Maybe you'd like another drink while you're waiting?'

'Maybe I would!'

The forensic laboratory rang the post as Alvarez was preparing to return home for lunch.

'The alcohol drunk was grape, not grain.'

Alvarez silently cursed his fate which forever seemed intent on wrapping the mantle of disorganization about him. It was murder, not suicide. Burnett had been drinking, but not from the bottle of whisky on the table. So either there had been a bottle of grape alcohol—coñac?—on the table and the whisky had been substituted for it, or there had been nothing because Burnett had had several drinks, but had not left the bottle out, perhaps obsessively tidy even

at such a moment. There could be no point in such a
substitution, so it was safe to say that there had been no
bottle on the table before the whisky had been put there to
give the impression of his having drunk to gain sufficient
careless courage to blow out his brains; placed by a man
who did not know that he disliked whisky or that he was
left-handed . . .

A technician rang soon after Alvarez had returned to the
office in the late afternoon.

'We've compared the two examples of typing. The type-
face is similar, but two different machines were used. There
are enough pertinent characteristics to make that quite
certain.'

One more corner of the pattern slotted into place.

The fingerprint department rang at half past seven.

'There are no dabs on the revolver but then, like I said,
there weren't going to be any.'

Experts were always so certain, Alvarez thought. Perhaps
that was what made them experts. 'And the bottle and the
glass?'

'Both wiped clean.'

'Thanks a lot.'

It was, surely, the clinching proof since it ruled out
the possibility—however remote—that before his death
Burnett had drunk whisky, perhaps as a gesture of contempt
aimed at himself. It was impossible to believe he would have
bothered to wipe down glass and bottle before committing
suicide.

Obviously, Alvarez decided—trying to find an excuse for
not doing so, and failing—he must ring Salas. But before
he did, it might be as well to fortify himself. He opened the
bottom right-hand drawer of the desk and brought out a
bottle of brandy and a glass and poured himself a generous,
and hopefully sustaining, drink.

The plum-voiced secretary said that Salas was in his office. It was not, Alvarez decided, his lucky day. 'Señor, Señor Burnett did not commit suicide, he was murdered.'

'Of course.'

'But why do you say that? I mean, I've only just been given the final proof . . .'

'The moment you assured me that beyond any shadow of a doubt he had committed suicide, I could be certain he had been murdered.'

CHAPTER 12

Alvarez looked at his watch and noted with pleasure that half the morning had passed. He settled back in the chair and stared without curiosity at the morning's mail which he had not yet bothered to open. Dolores was cooking Sopa Mallorquina for lunch. In the hands of a tyro, the vegetable and bread soup could resemble prison gruel, but in the hands of an expert it became a dish fit to be served on Mount Olympus. His sense of contentment blossomed. It was Saturday. Superior Chief Salas was so superior that he seldom worked on a Saturday afternoon and therefore there would be no need to cut short the afternoon's siesta . . .

Reluctantly he brought his thoughts back to the more immediate problem of Burnett's murder. There was really no case against Heal, although he was the only possible suspect at the moment; nothing to prove that the red Mercedes parked in the sitjola had been his, that he had returned late that night, or to suggest a possible motive. Phillipa Burnett had said that she had not recognized the voice of the man who had been arguing so angrily with her brother, but that was before a name could be given to the unseen person. Identification was an odd process and quite often it needed a trigger to set it off; a person's mind would be blank until prompted and then suddenly it became filled with details. Of course, to prompt could be to risk a false identification, but only if a person were easily misled and that did not describe the señorita.

Forty minutes later, he parked outside Ca'n Pario. Phillipa was out on the patio, reading, a glass on the wooden table by her side.

'You must have heard the bar open.'

'Señorita, I assure you I had no idea . . .'

'Of course not. How could you know that an old woman like me frequently risks perdition by drinking on her own? I was only pulling your leg. Sit down and tell me whether you'll change to red wine or stick to coñac?'

She stood, appearing ungraceful because her frock was voluminous and made her look very much larger than she was. She went indoors, returned with a tumbler which she handed him. She sat, suddenly slapped her left wrist with her right hand. 'The mosquitoes are voracious. I told that old fool, Tomás, that he'd lost all the fish in the estanque, but he wouldn't listen and now the mosquitoes are breeding like flies, if that's not rather Irish.'

'They are bad everywhere this year, señorita; even in the village we are plagued by them.'

'Well, you won't have come here to talk about mosquitoes. Has . . . Have you learned anything?'

'Perhaps, but I cannot be certain yet, which is why I'm here now to ask you something.'

'What?'

'Are you friendly with Señor Heal?'

'I've met him at parties, but I'd never say I was friendly with him. Frankly, he's the kind of person one has as an acquaintance, an amusing acquaintance, but not as a friend. My father used to say that a gentleman remained a gentleman even though he wore a cloth cap, a cad remained a cad even though he wore a topper.'

'You are saying that the señor is a cad?'

'That is what my father would have dubbed him; amusing, witty, but indisputably a cad. However, many of the other foreigners who live here find him a very nice man. It's all a question of standards.'

'Are yours the same as your father's?'

'I hope so. I believe that a man is who he is, not what he owns.'

'Did your brother know him?'

'Not to my knowledge. Justin, even when at his most gregarious, never liked cocktail parties.'

'He might, of course, have met him somewhere other than at a cocktail party?'

'Possible, but unlikely. Heal is welcomed by people who respect wealth, my brother was welcomed by those who respect honest intelligence. Why is this of any importance?'

'I have learned something which makes it likely that it was Señor Heal whom you heard at your brother's house on Monday morning.'

'Impossible.'

'How can you be so certain?'

'Heal's painfully cultured tones are unmistakable.'

'When a person is excited, he can sound different from normal.'

'I've been thinking about that voice. It's possible the speaker was a foreigner.'

'But Señor Heal is a foreigner.'

She started, looked disturbed. 'Yes, of course. I'm very sorry, that was a stupid thing to say. I do apologize.'

'Señorita, there is no need. All I was trying to do was to make certain what you meant.'

She ignored him. 'There is every need to apologize. As I say to anyone whom I hear complaining about the way something is done on this island, this is the Mallorquins' land and they can do things however they want and if a foreigner finds that objectionable, it's up to him to leave . . .

What I was trying to explain, very clumsily, was that the man spoke English with an accent; he was probably not a native Briton.'

'Could you suggest what nationality he might have been?'

'No.'

'You've definitely never heard him before?'

'Never.'

'Was there a second voice which might have been Señor Heal's?'

'No. Why do you keep mentioning him?'

'There was a red Mercedes parked in the sitjola.'

'So you mentioned before.'

'It was probably his.'

'All I can tell you for certain is that the man I heard was not Gerald Heal.'

He was too polite to point out that her quality of hearing might have deteriorated because of her age and he lacked the courage to suggest that, having once given her opinion, perhaps she was determined not to be seen to change it. And there was, of course, the faint possibility that another man had borrowed Heal's car or had been driven to the house by Heal . . .

Satisfied that there was nothing to be gained from further questioning, he settled back and enjoyed the brandy.

He returned to the office fifteen minutes before he could, in all honesty, leave to go home and enjoy the Sopa Mallorquina Dolores had promised. He decided to use up the time by telephoning Heal and demanding the other come to his office on Monday morning. On the face of things, any interview was not going to be easy because Heal was plainly a clever man. But clever men could make mistakes if they were over-conscious of their own cleverness.

He dialled Heal's number and the call was answered by Carmen. 'If the señor's in, tell him I'd like a word with him,' he said.

She gasped. 'But haven't you heard?'

'Heard what?' He hadn't an inkling of what could have happened, but instinct suggested his weekend was about to be ruined.

'The señor's been killed in a car crash.'

The mountains provided a different world from the coastal areas. Here, nature remained the ruler, powerful and antagonistic. Once, in some areas, there had been cultivation carried out along terraced slopes, but very few were now willing to labour so hard for so miserable a reward or to live in such isolation. One could drive for kilometres along tortuously zigzagging roads and not see a single inhabited building.

Fervently wishing he did not suffer from altophobia, Alvarez stood at the edge of the unfenced road and stared down at the crushed Mercedes which lay fifty metres down the very steep rock slope, hard up against a massive boulder. 'Was he dead when they reached him?'

'Too dead to say hullo.' The traffic policeman was young and determined to prove himself tough and unimpressionable. 'No one knew he'd gone over the edge until a couple of cyclists noticed that tree.' He pointed at a small pine whose trunk had been shattered when the car hit it immediately after leaving the road.

'Fancy cycling up here!'

'Preparing for the round-the-island race.'

They were welcome. 'What was the time?'

'They saw the car just before half past three in the afternoon. The dead man had a gold watch—they say that that must have cost a few hundred thousand pesetas!—which was broken and that had stopped at twenty-five past twelve.'

'Was he wearing a seat-belt?'

'No. Not that it would have done him much good if he had been, at the speed he must have been travelling.'

Alvarez turned to stare up at the very sharp left-hand bend roughly a hundred metres from where they stood. A reasonable judgement was that a prudent driver would not take that corner at more than thirty k.p.h. Obviously, Heal had come round it at a very much greater speed. Because he was the kind of man he was and in a powerful car? Or because quite suddenly he could not slow down? The car must have begun to slide. A skilful driver would normally have corrected the slide by using the wheel and maybe a mere dab of the brakes, an unskilled one would have panicked and slammed on the brakes as hard as he could. There were no marks on the road, proving the brakes had not been slammed on. Either the driver had overrated his skill or by then the car had been travelling so fast—at a speed not even a Finnish rally driver would contemplate—that no degree of skill could hold it on the road.

'You're going to have to get the car into Palma.'

'Are you loco? Get that wreck back up here, on to the road? How?'

'You're a bright bunch; someone will work out a way.'

'Look, a foreigner with plenty of booze inside him comes round a corner too fast, loses control, goes over the edge, and kills himself. That's his misfortune. And if the insurance company wants to look at things, that's up to them, but they can work out what to do.'

'I want the car taken to Traffic . . .'

'Then the order will have to come from someone a lot higher up the ladder than you are. We're not rupturing ourselves dragging that back up on to the road just on your say-so.'

Mustering what dignity he could, Alvarez returned to his car. He switched on the fan to clear the oppressive heat which had built up even though both front windows had been wide open, lit a cigarette, and stared across the wooded valley at the range of bleak mountains on the far side.

Heal had become a possible suspect in a murder case.
Now, he had died in a crash. Coincidence? Instinct and
experience suggested a connecting thread . . . The señorita
was convinced that the man she had heard in her brother's
house had not been Heal. But despite her refusal to accept
the fact, when a man was gripped by a violent emotion,
his voice could change in character and tone and become
difficult to recognize; the 'foreign' accent could well be no
more than evidence of such a change. The odds must be
that the car outside Burnett's home had been Heal's. A
strong-willed, highly successful man, certain of his own
superiority, he could have turned to murder more easily
than most. The very wealthy were often overtaken by the
I-am-God syndrome which led them to believe they had a
right to take any action that was necessary to ensure that
their will was done. It was realistic to envisage Heal as the
murderer of Burnett.

If Heal had murdered Burnett, he must have realized
that it was essential for his own safety that, since the police
had identified his car, he appeared to give them his full
and unstinted cooperation. Yet, knowing he had an eleven
o'clock appointment with the detective in charge of the case,
he had left the house beforehand and an hour and a half
afterwards had still been forty minutes' drive away. What
could have been so vitally important to him, if he was
the murderer, to make him prepared to take the risk of
antagonizing the detective?

Thirty minutes later he rounded one last hairpin bend to
reach the floor of a valley which led out to the central plain.
With no more precipitous drops to worry about, and only
light traffic, his mind returned to the case. If it was confirmed that the Mercedes's crash had been engineered, Heal
had been murdered. The two murders would surely have to
be connected, at the very least through their motives. Yet
he'd uncovered no motive for Burnett's death because it

seemed the only person who could benefit from that was his
sister; and not only had it been in her interests for the case
to be named the suicide it had first appeared to be, it was
almost impossible to believe her capable of fratricide. Even
if one stretched one's imagination to breaking-point, how
could her financial motive for her brother's death have any
connection with a motive for Heal's death? What could have
entwined the two men's lives when they were so totally
different in every respect and, it seemed, might never have
met?

Another twenty minutes' driving brought him to Llueso
and he crossed the torrente near the Roman bridge. He
parked outside the lottery shop, went in, and invested in six
entries in the primitive lottery. On the brief drive from there
to the office, he pondered the problem of how to spend the
hundreds of millions of pesetas one of his entries would
bring him.

He telephoned Salas. 'Señor Heal has been killed in a car
crash in the mountains and since he is the only possible
suspect in the murder of Señor Burnett—'

'Goddamn it, you do this deliberately!'

'But . . .' Alvarez became silent, accepting that his superior chief was incapable of appreciating the fact that he
had little or no say in the course events so often took. 'Señor,
in the circumstances it is essential that his car is examined
by Traffic to see if it was sabotaged.'

'I'm surprised you think it necessary to point that out.'

'But it is fifty metres down below the road and will be
very difficult to recover. Traffic are refusing to act without
an order from someone superior to myself.'

There was a long pause. 'Correct me if I'm wrong, but is
it not a fact that at the moment there is no hard evidence
to suggest whether the crash was the result of accident,
suicide, or murder?'

'That is so, señor. But the fact that Señor Heal had
become a suspect in Señor Burnett's murder suggests—'

'Suggests to someone of a rational mind, given to preferring simplicity to complexity, that if he were the murderer,
then on this drive he was either so mentally preoccupied
with the consequences of his crime that he did not exercise
the care so essential in the mountains or that he was overwhelmed by guilt and decided to commit suicide.'

'From what I've learned, he was a man so certain that
whatever he did was justified that he'd never have become
dangerously preoccupied or suffer that strong a sense of
guilt.'

'What motive is there for his murder?'

'I'm afraid I've no idea at this stage beyond the fact that
it must be connected with Señor Burnett's murder. But
I'm certain it will come to light in the course of future
investigations.'

'That, surely, will depend on who is doing the investigating? Very well, I'll give the order for the car to be retrieved.'
He rang off without another word.

Juan and Isabel were in the living-room, watching television. Alvarez settled in one of the free chairs and stared
at the screen, but soon lost interest in the heroic deeds of
the cartoon characters. Accept that the señorita was wrong
and that the man who had had a row with Burnett had been
Heal. What had the row been about? How could a retiring,
insignificant, weak-willed man so infuriate a brash, self-
important millionaire, whom he might never have met
before, that the latter became violently angry?

Something caught his attention and caused him to look
round. Dolores was standing in the doorway of the kitchen
and staring at him with an expression of deep concern. Why
was she worrying about him now? . . . And then he realized
why. Ever since it had been clear that he was dealing with
a case of murder, not suicide, he had been overwhelmed by
perplexing problems. But she, with a woman's instinct for
foolishly mistaking a man's emotions, believed that he'd

become so abstracted because he was yearning after Alma. Why would she never grant him emotional maturity?

As he pictured Alma, he experienced a resentful sadness; why did a man have to grow old?

CHAPTER 13

Traffic rang on Tuesday morning.

'We've examined the car from end to end. It suffered major damage in the fall, especially to the underside when this struck a very large boulder. As a result, while we can report that both brake lines ruptured, we cannot say for certain whether they had done so prior to the crash.'

'Does that mean you can't be certain whether someone sabotaged the car?'

'Officially, we can't; there's no conclusive evidence on that point. Unofficially, I will go so far as to say that we have found marks on the brake lines which do not seem to be consistent with impact forces. But understand this: I'm not saying that we're reasonably certain the car was sabotaged even if we can't supply the legal proof, I'm merely pointing out that it could have been.'

Alvarez thanked the other, rang off. So it was still imposs- ible to be certain Heal had been murdered, but instinct and logic said that he must have been. How to confirm instinct and logic? Uncover a motive for his murder and show that this motive was inextricably entwined with the motive for the murder of Burnett . . .

The laboratory reported less than an hour later.

'Death was due to severe crushing with resultant heavy damage to the brain and internal bleeding; death would have been virtually immediate. There were several areas of heavy bruising on the body, all consistent with the accident.

There was a deep wound in the right forearm, caused by a projecting piece of metal.

'The deceased had been drinking and the concentration of alcohol in the blood was approximately point one per cent.'

'How would that have affected him?'

'Impossible to be specific since each person's tolerance is different. But you could say he was in the delightfully dreamy state. If he was a regular, but by no means excessive, drinker, he would have been chatty, a little carefree, but probably nothing more obvious.

'What about his ability to drive?'

'One drink slows reactions slightly, several confuse them seriously. Up in the mountains, with switchback roads and hairpin corners, the amount he'd drunk would normally be called dangerous.'

After he'd rung off, Alvarez made some quick calculations. Because Heal had left his home relatively early, it seemed reasonable to suppose that he had not had any drinks before doing so. The bars in Laraix catered for pilgrims and bus tours, therefore were not likely to be the kind of places to which he would go. Then either he had had the drink with him in the car or whoever had earlier telephoned had brought it—with the aim of getting him sufficiently under the influence to dull his senses and miss or ignore any preliminary warnings of mechanical trouble in the car? Why would he have drunk so freely when he knew he had to return home and face a suspicious detective, probably made far more suspicious because he had failed to be there at the prearranged time?

Why had the murderer murdered? Because he knew Heal had murdered Burnett and in some way that knowledge threatened him? Because Heal knew that *he* had murdered Burnett? Because Heal knew why Burnett had been murdered?

Because the region was completely undeveloped, the drive into Costanyi sent Alvarez's mind back to his youth when

he'd worked in the fields, helping his parents, and at the
end of each day had been so tired he could hardly eat, even
though he was forever hungry.

He parked outside a bar, went in. By-passed by tourism
Costanyi might be, but inside there was a colour television
set, switched on throughout the day; at least there were no
space machines or juke boxes and his coffee and brandy cost
less than half what they would have done at a tourist bar in
the port. He asked the man who served him if he knew the
whereabouts of an English artist who lived nearby and, after
the man had spoken to his wife, was given rough directions.

He retraced his route to the outskirts of the village, then
took the first side road. The land was rocky and of very poor
quality and there was no irrigation, so that many of the
fields grew only almond trees, while there were belts of land
too rough even for them where grew only scrub bushes and
the occasional pine. Near one such belt, he disturbed a small
covey of partridges, something he had not seen for many
years.

The caseta, without electricity or telephone, was set in
the middle of a field. Outside were parked a Citroën 2CV,
which looked as if it had escaped from a breaker's yard, and
a white Ford Fiesta, on one rear window of which was
pasted the form which marked it as a hire car.

As he climbed from the Ibiza, a man stepped out of the
caseta. He shielded his eyes with his hand as he stared at
Alvarez, but made no move. Alvarez crossed the uneven
land. 'Señor Selby?'

'Well?'

'Is Señorita Heal here?'

'What's that to you?' he demanded with arrogant antago-
nism.

Hardly handsome, thought Alvarez critically and with a
certain satisfaction; features too heavy, expression too sullen, and dress too carelessly casual. 'If she is here, señor, I
would like to speak to her.'

'But what if she doesn't want to speak to you, señor?' Selby sneered.

'I am afraid that it is necessary, despite the great sadness she has suffered. I am Inspector Alvarez of the Cuerpo General de Policía.'

'A detective? . . . Are you the one she spoke to the other day?'

'That is so.'

'You asked her about Burnett. What's his death got to do with her now?'

'I will try to explain that when I speak with her.'

Selby hesitated, as if wondering whether to deny Alvarez's right to question Alma, then abruptly turned and went back into the caseta.

The other's manners, thought Alvarez, were not his strong point. Determined to show that a Mallorquin detective's manners were very much better, he called out: 'May I enter?' before he stepped inside. His first impression was that the main room of the caseta was so filled with a jumble of easels, canvases, paints, rags, bottles, books, and magazines that there was no room for humans. But a second impression identified an easy chair and a settee and a small table against the far wall just big enough to allow two people to eat at it.

Selby went through the doorway on the south side of the room, slammed the door shut behind him. As he waited, Alvarez examined those canvases which were facing outwards. Most of them featured landscapes, though a couple were of buildings only. The Mallorquin countryside, especially if gnarled, twisted olive trees were growing in it, was a favourite study for the dozens upon dozens of artists, amateur and professional, who lived on or visited the island. Although much of their work would have made a chocolate-box-maker cringe, some of it was attractive in an undemanding way. Selby's paintings, Alvarez reluctantly decided, were in a totally different league. His work possessed a quality, difficult to define but immediately recognizable, which added history, emotion, tragedy . . . He moved on, stepping around a cardboard box to look at another three canvases which were propped against the wall. When he could see the first one clearly, he drew in his breath with an audible hiss. Selby had painted a naked Alma with such sensuality that she was erotically alive. Alvarez experienced embarrassment and then anger; embarrassment because the picture fuelled desires, anger because here was a man so lost to decency that he'd painted a picture of her that others would leer over.

Selby returned and stood to one side of the doorway. Seconds later, Alma appeared. Her eyes were red and puffy and her hair needed brushing; she was dressed in shirt and jeans and the shirt was badly creased.

Alvarez, hoping she could not guess what he'd been looking at a moment ago, said: 'Señorita, I am deeply sorry about your very sad loss. I much regret disturbing you at such a tragic time.'

'Then why do it?' demanded Selby roughly.

She murmured something, looked appealingly at him and put her hand on his arm.

How could she give herself to such a coarse bear of a man? wondered Alvarez. For the modern generation, it seemed love was not simply blind, it was perversely blind.

'It's all right,' she said wearily. She moved forward and cleared the books and magazines off one of the chairs, motioned to Alvarez to sit.

Once settled on the chair, he became very aware of the fact that if he looked to his right, he would be able to see her naked portrait.

She cleared a space on the settee, sat. After a moment Selby joined her. He said: 'What's it you want to know?'

'First, I must tell the señorita something.'

'Why not tell her, then?'

'It is my very sad duty to have to say that it is possible that Señor Heal's crash was not an accident.'

Alma's voice was high. 'I don't understand.'

'The braking system on his car may have been tampered with in order to make him crash.'

'Impossible!' said Selby.

'Unfortunately, that is not so.'

'You're saying somebody deliberately killed him?' asked Alma.

'I am having to consider that possibility.'

'Oh my God!'

Selby leaned forward. 'That's a load of cod's. Gerry was driving like hell, as always, and went over the edge.'

So Selby knew that he had been a very fast driver! 'Señorita, at the moment there can be no certainty what happened. So now I have to ask you, can you name anyone who may have disliked your father so much that he would have wished to kill him?'

She shook her head.

'Please think about it very carefully . . .'

'She's just answered you,' interrupted Selby.

'Señor, since the known evidence is not yet conclusive, one way I can try to find out what happened is to discover whether there is someone who possessed a very bitter grudge against the señor. If there is such a person . . .'

'There isn't, so that answers that.'

'It really would be much better and quicker if you would allow the señorita to speak for herself. I have to know the answers to my questions and so the longer they take to answer, the longer I have to distress her.'

She looked up. 'But Guy's right. There really isn't anyone. I . . .' She stopped and tears welled out of her eyes and rolled down her cheeks.

'All right, that's enough,' shouted Selby. 'You can just clear off.'

Alvarez hesitated.

'I said, bloody clear off.'

Art had never been a favourite subject of his, thought

Alvarez as he stood, accepting the fact that it probably
would be best to leave. 'I am so sorry, señorita . . .'

'I'm . . . I'm all right now.' She brushed the tears away
from her cheeks.

'You're not all right,' contradicted Selby.

'I'd much rather get it over with. Don't you understand . . .'

'No, I bloody don't.'

'Perhaps,' said Alvarez, 'you have a reason for not wishing
the señorita to speak to me?'

Selby swore violently. He stood, hands bunched, heavy
face scowling, clearly longing to hit out and vent some of
his fury. Reason checked him. He turned, kicked out of the
way a book that had been lying on the floor, stamped out
through the front door.

She said: 'He . . . he sometimes gets very worked up.'

'So I would imagine, señorita.'

'I suppose it's what's called the artistic temperament.
And then he's had the terrible disappointment because of
the exhibition. That could have meant so very much to his
career. Please try and understand that he doesn't really
mean a lot of what he says, it's only his temper speaking.'

'I understand perfectly,' he answered gallantly and incor-
rectly. 'Señorita, this is very disturbing for you, so perhaps
it would be best after all if we talked another time?'

She shook her head.

He remembered Carolina's telling him that within her
character there was steel. The thought came that perhaps
in truth there was more steel than heart; he immediately
cursed his malign imagination. 'Then will you please think
again and tell me if there's anyone who could possibly have
disliked your father so much that he, or she, might have
wished to kill him.'

She did not answer for quite a time, then said: 'I just
can't believe there's anyone who could have hated him that
much.'

'Have you seen a great deal of him recently?'

'Quite a bit. Even though he and Guy . . . They didn't . . .' She stopped again.

'Didn't get on well together?'

'Gerry used to like Guy, perhaps because Guy was always prepared to say what he thought and stick up for what he'd said; Gerry respected strength and despised weakness. But when I came to live here . . . He could be incredibly old-fashioned for someone who lived a very liberated life.'

'Your father's attitude towards Señor Selby turned to one of dislike?'

'He said . . . What's it matter now what happened?'

He wondered if the possible implications of what she was saying were lost on her; or was it a case of clever artlessness being employed to try and suggest complete innocence? He decided to change the line of questioning. 'Señorita, when I saw you at your father's house, I explained that I wanted to ask him some questions. And I asked you if he could have been in his car in Llueso on Monday morning and you said no, he was at home all the time. But Carolina has told me that he always drove to Llueso, or the port, on a Monday morning to get an English Sunday paper. Why did you not tell me that?'

'Because . . .' She nibbled her lower lip. 'Because it was obvious you thought he might know something about Justin Burnett's death and that frightened me.'

'Why should it have done?'

'Gerry had been gritty for days and it was obvious that something was wrong. At first, I thought it was that woman.'

'That woman?'

'The Contessa Imbrolie.' Her tone had become scornful.

'But it was not?'

'It was nothing to do with her, as he told me in no uncertain terms. How he could ever have thought that she . . .' Her scorn gave way to distress. 'It doesn't matter now that it would have been a disastrous marriage. I wonder if she'll shed a single tear?'

'Does she know of your father's death?'

'I've no idea.'

'Where is she now?'

'She returned to Italy because of something to do with the house—or that's what she said. She never made any bones about preferring Italy to Spain and wanted Gerry to go and live with her there; he loved it here and expected her to move to the island. She'd have given him hell until he fell in with what she wanted. For someone as smart as he, it's incredible how blind he was to the kind of person she really is. I suppose it was the title. He had everything but an assured background. You wouldn't think that in these days anyone would have given a damn about that, but he did. He saw himself married to a contessa and couldn't see he'd also be married to someone with ice in her veins who wanted a tame poodle for a husband . . . God, you must think I'm a prime bitch!'

'Never, señorita.'

'It's just . . . What the hell!'

'Do you know her address and telephone number?'

'I think I've got them somewhere.'

'Would you give them to me?'

She nodded, went through to the bedroom; she returned, handed him a sheet of paper.

'Thank you. I will see that she is given the very sad news . . . When you learned that your father's unusual behaviour was not on account of the contessa, what did you think?'

'I stopped worrying and kind of forgot all about it until you mentioned Justin Burnett. Gerry . . . Well, he'd told me he was going to see Justin on the Monday morning and the way he was all tensed up made it clear it was important.'

'Did he mention why this should have been?'

'No. But since he didn't know Justin, there could have been only one reason.'

'What was that?'

'Because Justin was an expert in Greco-Roman artifacts.'

There were times, Alvarez decided, when one could be so blind that one failed to see a sign in fluorescent paint immediately in front of oneself. 'He needed some advice?'

'He must have done.'

'Can you say why?'

'I can guess. He had bought something from Simitis and wanted Justin's opinion of it.'

'Who is Señor Simitis?'

'Gerry occasionally bought things from him. He's a dealer in antiques. For my money, a dealer in antiques looted from graves. I can sense if anyone's basically rotten and he is. I warned Gerry, but he only laughed at me. He was so certain he was too clever to be taken in by anyone.'

'Does Señor Simitis live on the island?'

'He certainly has a house here, but I've no idea where.'

There were sounds from outside and Selby stepped into the room. He glared at Alvarez, his heavy chin thrust out. 'Then you're not finished?'

'Very nearly, señor . . . Señorita, I understand you were at your father's house on Thursday night. Did he mention either Señor Simitis or Contessa Imbrolie?'

She stared at him, her expression shocked.

Selby said loudly: 'She wasn't near her father's place on Thursday.'

'But her car was seen there and she was overheard . . .'

'I don't give a damn who saw or heard what. She was here all evening.'

Alvarez said sadly: 'Señorita, do you agree that that is the truth?'

She nodded.

He stood, his thoughts becoming even more bitter as he reviewed the possible reasons for her lie.

CHAPTER 14

Carmen led the way along one corridor, round a corner, and half way down another corridor. 'Here's the señor's study.'

Alvarez stepped past her to enter the large room, darkened because the shutters were closed. He opened the shutters as she left. The study looked out on to the courtyard and for a while he watched the fountain, whose jet seemed to cool the air even in the study. Then he turned. There was a large desk, two metal filing cabinets, a half-filled bookcase, a table with a word-processor and printer on it, and three shelves on which were stacked stationery. He crossed to the cabinets. It soon became clear that Heal had been a precise and tidy man when dealing with business affairs and all the papers were carefully filed. He removed any file, the title of which suggested the contents might interest him, put these on the desk.

One hour and forty-three minutes later he reached for the telephone, dialled. When the call was answered, he asked to speak to Señor Vilanova.

He identified himself. 'I'm investigating the death of Señor Heal . . .'

'Investigating it—why?'

'Because we cannot yet be certain of the cause of the crash.'

'Is that one way of saying it may have been deliberate and he was murdered?'

'It's one of the possibilities.'

The lawyer whistled.

'I want a word about his will. I have a copy of a Spanish one which you drew up and had registered in Madrid. Do you remember the contents?'

'Not off-hand.'

'The property on the island is owned by a company registered abroad and the will leaves his interests in the company to his wife and daughter in equal shares. Among his papers are two further wills and these deal, respectively, with assets held by nominee companies in other countries. Once again, the wife and daughter are sole beneficiaries. I've been able to make a very rough calculation of the total worth of the assets and the figure's nearly three billion pesetas.'

'As much as that! I realized he was rich, of course, but I'd no idea he was that rich.'

'Had he recently asked you to draw up a fresh will?'

'He said he was remarrying as soon as his divorce in England was granted and wanted to alter his bequests.'

'According to some handwritten notes, he intended to cut out his first wife and daughter and leave everything to his new wife.'

'As far as I can remember, that was the gist of things.'

'Could he legally cut out the two from his Spanish will?'

'As a foreigner and with the property owned by a company registered abroad, in practical terms the answer is that he could ignore the Spanish requirements to leave a proportion of his estate to his direct heirs and wife.'

'He could have disinherited both of them?'

'That's right. I remember now trying to persuade him to leave both the first wife and daughter a reasonable proportion of the estate, but he became quite angry and told me that if I wouldn't do the work, he'd find someone else who would.'

'But as far as you know, no further will has actually been drawn up and registered?'

'I certainly have not carried out the work.'

Alvarez thanked the other, rang off. He stared out through the nearer window at the fountain's jet. When he had asked

Alma about Thursday evening, she had been shocked to discover that he knew about her visit to Ca'n Heal. Selby had hurriedly given her an alibi and she had gratefully accepted the lie. People did not lie unless they had cause to do so . . .

Murder, as he was constantly reminding himself, normally called for a motive. A half-share in three billion pesetas was a motive that might strain a saint's rectitude.

It was easy to visualize Selby as a murderer. Given a motive, he would have little hesitation in sacrificing another man's life. Traditionally, artists were selfish; Selby would have been selfish whatever his trade. He needed success, and history showed that success had often not come even to a genius until too late . . . But in an age when the image was more valued than the substance, when the third-rate could be disguised as first-class by media exploitation, a painter with a great deal of money could promote himself into fame . . .

Alma was besotted by Selby—even to the extent that she allowed him to paint her in the nude. She had been described as having steel in her character; love and steel made a formidable combination. In the face of Selby's demands, had she agreed to go along with him in the murder of her father? . . .

Alvarez jerked his racing thoughts to a stop. He was forgetting. Since logic said that the two murders were connected, if Selby had no motive for murdering Burnett, it was unlikely he had murdered Heal. If he had not killed Heal, Alma had not condoned his actions and although she had rowed with her father the night before his murder and had lied to try and conceal that row her lie had nothing to do with her father's death.

Alvarez stood and walked over to the nearer window. The tinkling sounds of the water soothed his thoughts and made him realize how stupid it had been even to consider the possibility that a woman of Alma's character could be an accessory to her father's death.

Alvarez spoke to Pons, who was kneeling on a sack and working on a motor-mower just inside a large stone shed which stood a hundred metres from the western side of the house. 'Are you having trouble?'

'What's it look like?'

'Like you don't know very much about motor-mowers.'

Pons hawked and spat. 'No more I do, but the señor said that since I was the gardener, I mend the mowers. Wouldn't spend the money on getting the garage to do the work.'

'The richer they are, the more difficult they find it to spend.'

'Are you just bloody right! Every time the minimum wage goes up, it's a fight to get him to pay the extra . . .' He stopped as he remembered that Heal would resist no more wage increases. He was a short, stocky man, with a thatch of grey hair that stuck up at all angles above a weatherbeaten face.

'There was another chap working with you, wasn't there, who got the sack?'

'I told Frederico that's what would happen.' Pons grunted as he moved until he could stand. Something fell to the ground and it took several minutes, and much swearing, to find a small screw; he put this on the petrol tank of the mower. 'He's a young fool who's never learned to keep his head down. When a señor's paying the wages, he's always right. But Frederico had to assert himself and argue and didn't even have the sense to shut his mouth when the señor became really angry. "I'm entitled to my say." Look where that say got him!'

'Had he worked here long?'

'Less than a year. And you can call it work if you want, but I don't. He could make a quarter of an hour's job last half the day.'

'I suppose the sack upset his pride?'

'It did that all right and him and the señor had as good a shouting match as I've ever heard. Him in Spanish, the señor in English. Couple of daft buggers, not understanding what t'other was saying. Still, in the end Frederico understood one thing, right enough. He'd been sacked.'

'I imagine he lives locally?'

'Comes from the village, same as me.'

'Whereabouts in the village?'

Pons scratched the back of his thick neck with a dirt encrusted forefinger. 'Calle General Lobispo.'

As were so many villages in the interior of the island, Santa Lucía was built on a hill. When the Moors had been a constant threat, raiding small communities and sacking and slaughtering, a hill had offered both a vantage-point from which to gain an early warning and a certain degree of natural defence.

The streets were narrow and the inhabitants seemed unaware of that fact; as he entered a one-way street, Alvarez was almost run into by a woman on a Mobylette, travelling in the forbidden direction; when he was half way along, a child rushed out of the house and across the road and only by braking violently was he able to avoid a collision. The street led into a small square and he parked in the first available space, deciding that for once walking was preferable to driving.

The inhabitants of Santa Lucía seemed even more parochial than those of other villages and he became angrily certain that it was not mischance which caused him to be given the wrong directions to Calle General Lobispo three times—his speech marked him as being from the north and a forastero and therefore a person to be despised and, perhaps, even feared a little. He saw a Renault Five with the markings of the municipal police, parked outside a bar, and he went in. Two policemen, in their summer uniforms of light blue shirts and dark blue trousers, listened to him, then reluctantly admitted that the road he wanted was two up.

The road from the square was not steep, nevertheless by the time he reached Calle General Lobispo he was breathless. Perhaps, he decided, as he wiped the sweat from his forehead and face, he really should cut back on his smoking and drinking . . .

No. 14 was in the middle of a long row of side-by-sides which directly fronted the road; the shutters and door had been newly painted and three window-boxes were filled with climbing geraniums in different colours. The front door was open and he stepped through the bead curtain into the entrada, called out. A short, dumpy woman, with the aquiline features and dark complexion of Arab ancestry, entered from the room beyond. He introduced himself and said he wanted a word with her son.

She hesitated, gave him a look in which suspicion and dislike were mixed, left. There was only a short wait before Frederico entered. In his early twenties, he was dressed in a T-shirt which bore a message in English of such vulgarity it was certain his mother had no idea what it meant and the ubiquitous jeans. His features were similar to hers, but his complexion was even darker.

'You've heard that Señor Heal has been killed in a car crash?' Alvarez asked.

Frederico shrugged his shoulders.

'You haven't heard or you don't give a damn?'

'What's it matter which?'

'Quite a lot, if it turns out that his car was sabotaged.'

Frederico was shocked out of his sullenness.

'He sacked you last week. Did you decide to get your own back by killing him?'

His mother ran into the room. 'No!' she shouted. 'Never!'

Alvarez was not surprised to discover that she had

been listening; he would have been surprised had she not been.

'On my mother's grave I swear he couldn't do such a thing.' Her voice became shrill; gone, with all the volatility of the Mallorquin character, was the sullen resentment which she had previously shown and now she pleaded openly and with all her strength. 'Inspector, believe me. I beseech you, believe me.'

Frederico's fear was increased by his mother's. 'I wouldn't never do such a thing.'

'But you had one hell of a row with him when he sacked you?'

'Of course I did. I mean, he just didn't know what he was on about. Some plants can't do in the full sun and that's all there is to it, but all that silly bastard . . .' He stopped as he realized that in the circumstances his choice of words was unfortunate.

'What did you do after he sacked you?'

Frederico looked bewildered by the question.

'Where did you go?'

'I came back here, of course.'

'And then?'

'I went out.'

'To where?'

'To the bar.'

'How long were you there?'

'I . . . How do I know?'

She said: 'He was there all evening and when he came back he was so tight he couldn't go upstairs to bed and had to sleep down here.'

'Did you have a thick head in the morning?'

'I was bloody ill.'

'I told him,' she said. 'You drink like that and what d'you expect? I gave him some of my medicine, but it didn't do him no good.'

'When did you go out again?'

'Not until the evening.'

'Wouldn't eat any lunch,' said his mother. 'I said to him, why go and drink . . .'

Alvarez only half listened to her. If they were telling the truth, Frederico had had no hand in the death of Heal.

CHAPTER 15

Because the telephone directory was divided into towns and villages, it was necessary to know where a subscriber lived before one could find his name in the alphabetical list; Spaniards found the system logical, foreigners saw in it yet one more proof that Spain was separated from Europe by more than the Pyrenees. Alvarez began his search with Palma, ten minutes later found the entry he wanted under Sant José. Gerasimos Simitis lived in Ca'n Kaïlaria. Should have been Ca Na Kaïlaria, he thought pedantically as he shut the directory. He checked the time. If he left now to drive to Sant José, which lay beyond Palma, he could not arrive before seven—his siesta had been rather a long one —and there would be no hope of returning home until well after nine . . . The evening was not a good time to question a man; far better leave it until the morning.

Because of clever salesmanship, the urbanizacíon of Sant José was known internationally as a haven for the rich; one could own a house there, or visit friends, and when back in Britain remark on the fact without apologizing for having gone slumming. Lots of lovely people owned property there; a few pleasant ones did as well.

Alvarez braked, turned off the road and drove slowly up the gravel path to come to a stop in front of an elaborate porch. He climbed out of the car. The house was typical in that it lacked any architectural imagination, had asymmetrical roof lines, and was poorly built, but it was very large and in such a situation was probably worth a hundred million pesetas. He rang the bell and, as he waited, stared at the view. Because he was on rising land the sea was clearly visible, almost as brilliantly blue as computer-enhanced travel posters would have it. He revised his estimate up to a hundred and twenty million. Foreigners always paid extra to be in sight of the water. Yet when he'd been young, to live where the sea could see one had been held to be unlucky; perhaps because so many fishermen lost their lives.

A maid, young and with a slender body, but with heavy features which culminated in a bulldog jaw, opened the door. She showed him into a room to the right of the high-ceilinged entrance hall and this, because of the way in which it was over-furnished rather than for its contents, reminded him of the larger sitting-room in Heal's house.

Less than two minutes later a man hurried in, one hand held out. 'Inspector Alvarez, a pleasure to meet you.' His Spanish was only just accented. He shook hands with enthusiasm. 'Please sit down. And you will permit me to offer you some refreshment?'

Alvarez liked to boast that he never judged until he knew the whole man, yet honesty compelled him to admit that he did not always live up to his own boast. Because a man had wavy dark hair—styled, dyed?—a pampered skin that clearly received constant attention, a mouth which smiled too hard, because he dressed with such elegance, and tried to be so welcomingly pleasant, were not good reasons to dislike him on short acquaintance. He disliked Simitis on sight.

'I can offer you coffee, tea, a very delicious tisane, whisky, gin, brandy . . .'

'A coñac, thank you, with ice.'

'Cognac, armagnac, Spanish brandy, or Javito from Hungary which is little known, but which I can highly recommend?'

'One of the local brands will do fine.'

Simitis crossed to the near wall, with a skipping movement, and pressed a bell. 'Please do sit down, Inspector. As they say where I was born, a man who stands keeps his head nearer heaven, but his feet grow tired.'

The only chairs, gilded, looked as if any weight of consequence would fracture their gracefully curved but spindly legs. Alvarez hesitated.

Simitis made a sound that was half-way between a high-pitched laugh and a giggle. 'They are very much stronger than they appear. Only last week, a lady who weighs perhaps twice—no, let me be tactful, one and a half times—as much as you, settled on one without any disastrous results.'

As Alvarez sat, carefully, despite the assurance, the maid entered. Simitis asked her to bring the drinks. After she'd left, he crossed to an ornately inlaid clover-leaf table and picked up a silver cigarette box. 'Do you smoke? These are Virginian, these Turkish; those are for Parisians who are nostalgic for the scent of the metro, and those are made for me by a man in Athens who used to supply the Royal Family before they were so ungraciously rejected.'

Alvarez chose one of the Athens cigarettes. It proved to be made from the smoothest of smooth tobaccos.

Simitis sat. 'Now, to what do I owe the honour of this visit?'

'I'm investigating the murders of Señor Burnett and Señor Heal.' He spoke with deliberate bluntness, hoping to pierce Simitis's egregiously fulsome manner. He was disappointed.

'You are saying that both were murdered?'

'I am.'

'My God!' He clapped his palm to his forehead. 'Shocking! Abominable! A nicer, more talented man than Señor Heal one could not hope to meet. Sadly, there is much truth in the saying, The gods envy youth because that is the one gift they cannot grant themselves. And like mere mortals, that which they envy, they destroy . . . But I digress. You are investigating two shocking murders. How can I help you? Ask me anything. Nothing would give me greater satisfaction than to bring to justice the wicked person responsible.'

Before Alvarez could say anything, the maid returned with two crystal glasses on a silver tray. She handed one glass to Alvarez, the other to Simitis, left.

Alvarez drank. The quality of the brandy suggested that it was Carlos I. 'Did you know Señor Burnett?'

'I met him once, perhaps eighteen months ago. I had a small Roman brooch which I believed dated from the first century BC, but a self-styled expert insisted was from the second century AD. Knowing that Señor Burnett was an even greater expert on Greco-Roman artifacts than on eighteenth-century paintings, I arranged to meet him and ask him for his verdict. He agreed with me.'

'You haven't seen him since?'

'No, although quite recently I did put a small commission his way as a mark of my respect for his scholarship. Perhaps you know his book on Roman body armour?'

'I don't.'

'If you ever have the chance, read it. The breadth of scholarship is outstanding. And now the poor man can write no more. Clio has lost a great disciple. And he was murdered! How vile men's actions can be! How true that the tragedies of life lie in the past, not the future, because the past cannot be altered.'

Alvarez hastened to check the flow of words. 'You also knew Señor Heal?'

'Indeed. How can one adequately express one's grief at the thought of such a loss?'

'How well did you know him?'

'A question which, like so many, has two sides. The first is largely a philosophical one. Can one man ever know another well? When it is extremely difficult to be certain what one's own reactions will be under all possible emotional states and all possible circumstances? But it is the obverse side which I am sure you are interested in. How close a relationship with Señor Heal was I honoured with? Can I suggest any reason for his being killed? Can I name someone so wicked, so lost to all decencies, he might have carried out the dastardly act?'

Alvarez's dislike for the other flourished. Beneath the endless flow of words there was mockery. Simitis looked with scorn on a detective in crumpled clothes who so clearly was unused to Carlos I brandy and royal cigarettes.

'I will try to answer the questions. My relationship with Gerald Heal began as a business one; but I pride myself that it soon blossomed into friendship. He was a man I greatly admired, both professionally and privately.'

'What business did you have with him?'

'From time to time I sold him works of art; works of the finest quality.'

'You're a dealer?'

'You may call me that. I buy from those who seek money and sell to those who seek beauty. I think of myself as a benefactor.'

'From whom and where do you buy?'

'Inspector, Inspector, what a question! Every trade has its little secrets.'

And his secrets would not bear the light of day. 'Had you recently sold Señor Heal something?'

'Indeed.'

'What?'

'Part of Priam's treasure. Resurrected a second time!' He giggled. He drank, drew on the cigarette. 'You naturally know the history of that treasure?'

'Just remind me.'

Simitis brought a mauve silk handkerchief from his trouser pocket, wiped his lips, replaced the handkerchief. 'King Priam, son of Laomedon, ruled over Troy at the time of the Trojan War. When Troy fell, he was slain. So Homer told us. Nonsense, said the experts. Homer was not one bard, he was many, the *Iliad* and the *Odyssey* were written centuries after the events they were supposed to depict, and the stories were myths; no Troy, no wooden horse; Priam had not taken charge of the body of his son, Hector, killed by mighty Achilles; Odysseus had not wandered for ten years while Penelope wove and unwove; Agamemnon had not survived the war only to return home to be murdered, and his son, Orestes, had not in revenge murdered his mother and her lover.

'One man refused to believe the experts. He said there had been a Trojan War, as Homer had declared. Since he was not a scholar, but a businessman, he was ridiculed. But Heinrich Schliemann was crazy enough to spend his own money in search of Troy and because the gods love madness, they led him to Troy. He excavated the city and found King Priam's palace and finally King Priam's treasure. (Or so he claimed. Experts say it was not heroic Troy he found, but an earlier city; the treasure dated from before King Priam's time. Why should one believe them now, when they have been proved so wrong before?)

'There were silver vases and knives, gold diadems, earrings, and thousands of gold rings and buttons. What to do with this fabulous treasure? Schliemann smuggled it out of Turkey and later presented it to the German government. In the last World War, during the time that Berlin was occupied by the Russians, the collection disappeared and from that day to this it has never been seen again. Does it still exist? Almost certainly not. In an act of unsurpassed and unsurpassable vandalism, the gold and silver was melted down and sold for what it would fetch—a millionth of what the treasure had been worth.'

'You said you sold Señor Heal a part of the treasure. How could you do that when you've just told me it disappeared?'

Simitis giggled. 'Trust a detective to point that out!'

'You sold him a fake?'

'Of course.'

'You admit it?' Alvarez could not hide his surprise. He'd have said that Simitis was the last man willingly to admit he was a swindler.

'Inspector, do you imagine that I alone know the facts? Everyone with the slightest breath of romance in his breast knows them; every lover of the heroic past longs to be told that the collection has been recovered; every heart which beats with cupidity dreams of rediscovering the treasure. From the beginning of my love-affair with the past, I have been offered pieces from King Priam's treasure. Travel east through Turkey and in village after village there will appear a button or a ring from it. Peasants in Armenia, Azerbaijan, Georgia, Dagestan, Kabardino-Balkar, will show you pieces and ask so many roubles that the head spins. All are fakes. Most are crude and could deceive only a naïf who wishes to be fooled, but very, very occasionally such a piece is a work of art and it is the man who made it who is the naïf because he is an artist and could make a fortune if he worked legitimately. One such piece, a gold diadem, was offered to me a few months ago by a Kurd. He swore by all his ancestors that it was genuine and could not believe that I was not to be fooled. The price descended from the realms of romance to the point where I decided that for such a modern work of art, which this was, it was not excessive. I paid him what he was then asking. And the poor fool was as delighted as having bamboozled me as with the money I gave him.

'I brought the diadem back and had it here, mounted on a square of crimson velvet set on the mantelpiece. It was so beautiful that it was possible to believe a miracle had come to pass and the treasure of King Priam had, in truth, been rediscovered.'

Alvarez looked across at the mantelpiece above the large open fireplace, and visualized the gleam of gold against the

crimson background. He tried to remember exactly what a
diadem was.

'Señor Heal dined with me one evening. As was to be
expected, when he entered the room, his attention was
immediately drawn to my new acquisition. He asked me
about it. I teased him and said that it was from King Priam's
treasure . . . But it was not a joke that could last because
he was a man not only of taste, but of excellent judgement.
So I soon admitted that it was a fake since I did not want
him to suspect me of trying to fool him. Later, he said he
wanted to buy the diadem. I refused because I had grown
to like it very much. You see, although I naturally always
want the genuine article, if that is impossible I am content
to possess a fake which is as perfect as the original and
only lacks its years. He would not accept my refusal, but
demanded I name a price. A man who makes his living
from buying and selling cannot afford to buy but not sell
simply because his emotions are involved. Nevertheless, I
named a very high price, consoling myself with the thought
that if he agreed, not only would I make a handsome profit,
I could always return to my seller and ask for another copy
to be made. Señor Heal paid me what I'd asked. Never have
I regretted a deal more.'

'Regretted or rejoiced?'

'I do not understand.'

'It's my guess you rigged the whole set-up.'

Simitis smiled, but his dark brown eyes expressed hostility. 'You are very direct. Some might even call you rude.'

'Possibly.'

He stood, hurried out of the room with his restricted,
skipping stride.

Alvarez finished his drink. It had been a standard confi-
dence trick, playing on another man's greed and conceit,
carried out by an expert. The diadem had been displayed
in a manner that must attract Heal's attention. He'd examined it. Then Simitis had laughingly confessed that it

was a fake. But was it really a fake? An extremely self-confident man, ready to believe himself far cleverer than he was, Heal had become convinced that the diadem was of such superb workmanship that it had to be genuine and it was Simitis who was mistaken. So Heal had decided to buy this fake, believing it to be genuine, and had eagerly paid several times what it was worth, silently laughing at the man who, unknown to him, was laughing at him . . .

Simitis returned with a sheet of paper. 'This is a copy, Inspector. Naturally, should it ever become necessary, I can produce the original.'

It was a photocopy of a receipt, signed by Heal, for a modern reproduction in gold of a Trojan diadem. The price had been fifty thousand pounds. Alvarez handed back the copy receipt.

'Would you now like to withdraw the ridiculous allegation you made earlier?'

'There are two ways of suckering a man. The easier is to fool him into believing something is genuine when it is a fake; the more difficult is to fool him into believing it is genuine, but that you, the person trying to sell it, have not the wit to realize that it is genuine.'

'The receipt proves that I did not fool him.'

'It shows that it would be very difficult to prove you did.'

'Perhaps you should remember, Inspector, that I have friends in high places.'

Alvarez was about to reply that so did monkeys, but checked the words. Sadly, it was probably true that Simitis did know important people with considerable influence. Even though Spain was now a democracy, a mere inspector was easily disposed of . . .

'And now, since I have important business to conduct, perhaps you'll excuse me?'

Alvarez stood. 'Before I leave, señor, I have to ask two more questions. Where were you on the thirteenth of this month? That was a week ago last Monday.'

'Why should the answer be of any interest to you?'
'It is the day on which Señor Burnett died.'
'You think it might have been I who killed him?'
'I have to consider all possibilities.'
Simitis went over to the right-hand of two small, matching desks, opened the flap, picked up a diary. He flicked through the pages. 'I was in Madrid. A man of your suspicious disposition will no doubt wish to verify that, so I suggest you ring the Hotel Don Pepe. What is the second question?'
'When you mentioned Señor Burnett earlier on, you said you'd met him once and later on had put a small commission his way. What does that mean?'
'My business has brought me into contact with a multitude of people connected with art, in the broadest sense, most of whom are, I am happy to say, prepared to accept that I am an honest man. One such person is Señor Joan Pravos, the owner of Galerías Mugar, one of the major art galleries in Barcelona. He mentioned to me that he needed an expert's opinion on the work of an artist who lived on this island. I am interested in paintings but certainly no expert on them so I suggested he contact Señor Burnett who, as you may know, was interested in paintings before he turned to Greco-Roman artifacts.'
'Who was the artist in question?'
'I have forgotten his name.'
'Could it have been Guy Selby?'
Simitis shrugged his shoulders.
'What was Señor Burnett's judgement on the paintings?'
'I have no idea.'
Alvarez thanked the other for his help, managing not to sound too sarcastic. Simitis did not shake hands.
Back in the Ibiza, Alvarez started the engine, made a three-point turn, drove down to the gateway. A couple of cars passed and then he was free to draw across the road and start the journey back through Palma to Llueso.
Some things were becoming clearer, others more opaque.

Heal had bought the diadem, having been cunningly bamboozled into believing it to be genuine. He had taken it to
Burnett for verification, but Burnett had declared it to be
the fake that Simitis had named it. A man who believed
himself to be extremely clever, bolstered in such belief by
his great wealth, contemptuous of less fortunate people,
Heal had been desperate to evade the truth. Illogically, he
had vehemently argued with Burnett, trying to make the
other reverse his judgement; perhaps he had even tried
bribery.

Yet however certainly the facts now identified Heal as
being the person who'd rowed so fiercely with Burnett,
Phillipa flatly denied it could have been he. How to make
sense of this? Was he missing something vital? If so, what
on earth could that something be?

CHAPTER 16

Inspector Magnasco rang Alvarez from Sienbasso. He spoke
in Italian, Alvarez answered in Spanish, and both were
perplexed. By mutual agreement, they switched to English.

'I go contessa's house and I speak servants,' said the
inspector, whose English was not of Linguaphone standards.
'He is not there.'

'What's that?'

The Italian inspector spoke rapidly and after a moment's
bewilderment, Alvarez appreciated the fact that the other
switched genders and 'he' was the contessa. It seemed that
over the past fourteen months, the Contessa Imbrolie had
had a handsome male friend, considerably younger than
herself; her friend had a passion for gold trinkets and fast
cars. On her sudden and unexpected return from Mallorca,
she had found him in the company of a young woman of
extraordinary beauty. There had been a fierce row, following

which the beautiful young woman had left, the handsome
male friend had swapped his three-year-old Alfa Romeo for
a new Porsche, and the contessa and he had gone on holiday
to the Seychelles, leaving the Tuesday before Heal's crash.

Say one thing for the rich, Alvarez thought, their lifestyles
were different.

He dialled the Hotel Don Pepe and spoke to the assistant
manager. An hour later the assistant manager rang back.

'One of the waiters served Señor Simitis dinner in his
suite on Monday evening.'

'Does he know what time this was?'

'Near enough to nine o'clock.'

'Thank you very much for your help.'

He replaced the receiver. If Simitis had been in Madrid
at nine o'clock, it was extremely unlikely that he could have
been in Llueso at midnight.

Salas said, over the telephone: 'Let me make quite certain
that I understand. You are requesting permission to fly to
Barcelona in order to question the owner of an art gallery;
the reason for this request being that you believe he may be
able to help with your investigations?'

'Yes, señor,' replied Alvarez.

'Yet when I ask in what way may he be able to help, you
cannot give a reason.'

'In this particular case, it is rather difficult to explain . . .'

'My impression is that in every case you undertake, you
find it difficult to explain. Presumably, the gallery owner
knew Señor Burnett?'

'I rather doubt it.'

'Then he knew Señor Heal?'

'I don't think so.'

'Has he recently visited this island?'

'I've no reason to think he has.'

'Then how can he possibly be in a position to assist you?'

'The thing is, in the course of my inquiries his name has cropped up.'

'And that is reason enough to visit him? Then perhaps I should hope that the next name which crops up is not one belonging to a person who lives in New Zealand.'

'I have a feeling that he is important.'

'You have a feeling? That is different! Everything is explained!'

Sometimes a hunch . . .' He trailed off into silence.

Salas spoke wearily. 'I can see only one solution. Follow your hunch and fly to Barcelona. But you will make the journey in the most economical way possible and you will not present the cost of a meal at the Ritz on your expense sheet. Is that quite clear?'

'Yes, señor.'

The connection was cut.

Alvarez had begun to sweat and he used a handkerchief to mop his face and neck. It had been a very close run thing and there had been a moment when he'd thought that he was going to have to name Selby. To have done so would have been to implicate Alma. And although he accepted that love could make a strong woman weak, he still fought against the possibility that love could have forced her to condone her father's murder.

Dolores, standing by the side of the dining-room table, stared with consternation at Alvarez. 'You're . . . you're going to Barcelona tomorrow?'

He nodded.

'Santa María!' she murmured. Unexpected happenings always disturbed her; she liked today to be yesterday, tomorrow to be today.

'I'll be back in the evening.'

'You're returning the same day!' This made her even more upset. By her standards, a trip to Palma was still a major event; to set out to make the return trip to Barcelona in one day was almost to challenge the Almighty.

'You look as if you need a drink to cheer yourself up.' He expected her to refuse, but she didn't. Hastily, he poured out two brandies and went through to the kitchen for ice.

She took one glass from him and drank. Then she looked at him, her lustrous dark brown eyes filled with concern. 'Enrique, it's because of her that you're going to Barcelona and returning on the same day, isn't it?'

'In one sense, yes; but not in the way you're thinking.'

'No? I'll tell you exactly how I'm thinking. That a woman's heart is pierced by thorns when she sees a man who she loves making a fool of himself; when she can see the precipice which lies ahead of him, but he cannot; when she shouts a warning, but he closes his ears. I am thinking that when he has fallen and wounded himself, it is not the woman who lured him to the fall on whom he calls for help, but it is to the woman whose warning he refused to heed.'

'You've got it all wrong.'

'Is it really that easy to forget all the times in the past that I have seen you blinded by a chit of a woman?'

'You've been watching too many soap operas. It's nothing like that.'

'It is exactly like that every time a man lusts after a woman.'

'I'm not lusting and have another drink and stop seeing everything in terms of high tragedy.' He drained his glass, stood, held out his hand and without a word she handed him her glass.

When he returned, he said: 'You can tell me. Can a woman be made evil by love?'

Her indignation was immediate. 'Only a man could ask so stupid a question! If a woman is loved—if there is any man left who can love and not lust—she is made good, not evil.'

'There have been women who have done terrible things because of love.'

'Because of lust.'

'Can you ever really separate the two?'

'A woman can always separate them.'

'The señorita is a woman who can love deeply. Yet the evidence is suggesting that the man she lives with may have committed a very great evil. If she loves him deeply, could she because of that condone his evil even though knowing it to be evil?'

She had only listened to part of what he had said. 'She lives in sin with another man, yet you still lust after her?'

'Can't you understand that I've never lusted after her? That was all in your imagination.'

'The yearning in your eyes was not imagination.'

'Despair, not yearning; despair because although my heart tells me she's innocent, the facts suggest more and more strongly that she shares the guilt.'

He had been speaking calmly, without the bitter emotion there surely would have been had he been vainly in love with the chit of a foreign woman. She experienced a sweeping sense of thankfulness which had to find expression. She would, she decided, prepare something special for supper.

He spoke quietly, his tone uncertain. 'Sometimes I don't know what my job really is. Am I just a servant of the law or am I a small part of justice?'

She would buy some jamón serrano.

'If I am the former, I should not concern myself with the consequences of what I do; the measure of those must be someone else's responsibility. But if I am the latter, I must worry and if I can see they may cause an injustice, I must do everything in my power to avoid that happening.'

She still had time to cook a piece of lomo.

'If all the facts point in one direction, but one believes the sign they give has to be wrong, how justified can one be if one ignores them? Is failure to apprehend the guilty as great an injustice as the apprehension of the innocent? How far can one be blamed for one's own weaknesses? I can say that you must never be guided by evil, but you may not be as strong as I and therefore cannot fight it as hard. Do I really have the right to blame you when through no fault of your own you cannot meet my standards?'

The larger of the nearby bakeries might have an ensaimada con crema Catalan; the whole family loved them.

'Suppose I uncover the final piece of evidence which identifies her man as the murderer, can I even begin to justify the withholding of that evidence because I am so certain that she could never willingly follow evil and I know that if he is accused, so must she be, if not as a principal, then as an accessory?'

She said: 'I must go out to the shops and buy some food for supper.'

Only an incompetent detective would ever imagine there could be answers to such questions.

As the plane gathered speed on the take-off, Alvarez, his eyes tight shut, decided that he'd rather be in the centre of the Palma bullring, caping a seven-hundred-kilo bull with unshaven horns, than where he was. But beyond a dangerous rumble from the undercarriage as this was raised, nothing happened and eventually he opened his eyes, deciding that perhaps he was to be allowed to live a little longer. He tried to catch the attention of an air stewardess, to persuade her to serve him a very large brandy even though the flight lasted only half an hour.

His knowledge of Barcelona was scanty (he had visited the city only twice before), but he knew that the inhabitants would be united in their desire to swindle him. When he left the old terminal building at the airport and climbed into a taxi, he made certain the meter was starting at zero and he closely watched the route they took into the city, even though he had no idea which was the shortest.

The traffic was little denser than it was during the rush hour in Palma, yet it seemed to bear down on him until he wanted to tell the driver to slow, but the latter appeared to be practising for the Spanish Grand Prix; the buildings were little taller than those in Palma, yet they seemed to become skyscrapers which choked off all clean air . . .

They turned on to the Diagonal, then off it, and abruptly they were in a world that was welcomingly familiar; people had time to sit at pavement cafés, a city employee, brushing down the pavement, leant on the broom and contemplated either infinity or a crack in the pavement, a state policeman placidly watched a car park in front of a Parking Prohibited sign, and a gipsy woman, too tired to beg, sat on the pavement, leaned against a wall, and closed her eyes.

The taxi came to a halt. He climbed out, checked the meter-reading, and gave a tip that on the island he would have considered over-generous. He was unsurprised when the driver sneered at his parsimoniousness.

The gallery had a single show window and in the centre of the display area stood an easel on which was a large canvas that, to his Philistine eyes, depicted the track of an inebriated spider. He went inside. The paintings along the walls suggested more busy spiders while small sculptures, set on pedestals, lacked even that much definite form.

The gallery was L-shaped and there was a desk set at the point where the two arms joined, behind which sat a woman of indeterminate age. He introduced himself and said he wanted to speak to the owner of the gallery. Being a cultured Catalan, she would have liked to have misunderstood his Mallorquin, but was inhibited from doing so by the knowledge that he was a detective. She said she'd find out if Señor Pravos were free. She went through the doorway behind the desk, returned almost immediately. 'He can spare you a moment.'

The office was large and very elegantly furnished. Pravos was small and very elegantly turned out. His black hair was styled, his hands manicured, and his recently pressed linen suit was of the same delicate shade of blue as the wallpaper. There were three rings on his fingers, but none in his ears.

He made Alvarez feel lumpenly dressed, despite a clean shirt that morning. When he shook hands, the feel of his skin was like soaped silk. 'My assistant says you're a detective from the Baleares?'

'From Mallorca.'

'Then sit and tell me, what brings a detective from the Island of Calm to this temple of art?'

Alvarez sat in front of the large desk, on which stood a small sculpture of priapic origins. 'I believe you're friendly with Señor Gerasimos Simitis?'

'I am acquainted with him, certainly. Why do you ask?'

'Because I need to know more about him. Is he honest?'

Pravos was disconcerted. 'You're clearly a man for whom the world is a place of definite values! Shall I say this: I am certain he is quite incapable of stealing any of the paintings in this gallery.'

'You asked him about the work of an artist who lives on the island?'

'That is correct.'

'Why did you do that?'

'The matter is confidential.'

'Not when you're talking to me.'

'Very well, I will tell you. I am a man of considerable taste and judgement, possessed of a desire to lead the public towards the light. It is part of my mission to introduce art to the ordinary man in the street, to switch on a torch in his mind and soul; another part of such mission is to discover artists whose worth has not yet been recognized and to introduce them to the newly-born art lovers. Sadly, the tasks are not easy. The ordinary man is unadventurous as well as ignorant and can only be persuaded into fresh realms when his curiosity is aroused by some form of publicity. I championed a certain artist for no little time, but without success, until it was decided that he would gain publicity by setting out to break the world record for pole-squatting. Of course he failed to equal St Simeon's forty-five years;

nevertheless, since he was a native of this city, he received considerable publicity and people came to view his work and to buy it.

'Lacking such initiative an artist can, of course, gain the necessary publicity by a judicious use of money. One may bitterly regret that the world in which we live is a commercial one, but one cannot escape that fact and so when I was approached by a totally unknown artist who requested an exhibition for which there would be full financial backing, I was ready sympathetically to examine his work. It proved to be of a character which normally does not attract me, yet it unmistakably displayed talent. I agreed to his request. Later, it appeared that the gift of sponsorship had been withdrawn. I was left with no alternative but to cancel my offer.

'I then received a visit from a young lady who vehemently demanded that, despite the loss of financial backing, I honour my promise of an exhibition. On my pointing out that the financial situation made this impossible, she replied that art was not to be measured in pesetas . . .' He sounded surprised. 'She was a very persistent young lady; quite un-Spanish. And in order to gain relief from her vehemence I was forced to admit that I had seen merit in the artist's work and I would like to hold an exhibition of it, but I added that it was necessary to gain some form of pre-exhibition publicity. En passant, I mentioned the artist who had attempted, but failed, to win the record for a pole-squat. Regrettably, she failed to appreciate that this was an example, not an instruction, and began a tirade on art and Mammon . . . Let me confess, Inspector, that things reached such a pass that in order to regain some peace I promised that if I thought that despite a lack of advance publicity there was a chance of the exhibition being success-ful, I would after all hold it. I don't think I have ever before met anyone of such fierce and pugnacious deter-mination . . .

'Not long afterwards, I was talking to Señor Simitis, with whom I have occasionally done a little careful business, and I mentioned my problem and asked if he knew the artist's work. He didn't, but suggested that if I wanted a further opinion on it, I should speak to Señor Burnett, who lived on the island.

'I telephoned Señor Burnett and offered him a small commission to contact the artist, look at his work, and judge it. He agreed to this after making it clear that it was years since he'd dealt with paintings and that then his interests had lain with the eighteenth century.

'His report was brief, but explicit. He didn't particularly like the work, yet he had little doubt that the painter had an unusual talent. But he thought the quality of the work to be a subtle one and unlikely to be recognized at first sight by the ordinary person. In the face of such a report I naturally had to bring to an end any possibility of an exhibition.'

'Who was the artist?'

'I forget his name, but it will be in the records.' He stood, went over to a filing cabinet, slid out the top drawer, and searched through the papers. 'Guy Selby,' he said, having difficulty in pronouncing both names.

CHAPTER 17

The tapas bar ran for three-quarters the length of the long, narrow space; in the last quarter were half a dozen tables for those who preferred not to eat at it. Alvarez made a final choice of a portion of baby octopus in a piquant sauce, carried the plate, a glass of white wine, knife and fork, over to the only vacant table.

He ate, his mind far away. It must have appeared to Selby that Burnett had scorned his work and ruined his chances of an exhibition that might well have made his name and ensured fame and fortune. So here was a motive for his murder—the revenge of the artist whose pride was not to be measured by normal, logical standards. And since Burnett had been murdered, there could be little doubt but that Heal's death had been murder and here was the motive of a fortune, to be gained through Alma, which would be lost if Heal lived to marry the contessa. Only Selby had a motive for both murders . . . How could there be the slightest justification for continuing to withhold his name from the superior chief? Yet once he was named as the prime— the only—suspect for both murders, inevitably Alma must be implicated . . .

He finished the plateful of mixed fish, prawns, mussels, octopus, squid, and berberechos and then returned to the bar for a second course of liver, kidneys, meatballs, diced pork, and garlic stew. He asked for a glassful of red wine.

Back at the table, he resumed eating and thinking. When he returned home, he would have to report fully to Salas. As a consequence, Selby and Alma would be questioned vigorously and probably be arrested. The thought of Alma suffering the degradation of jail made him feel as if about to choke . . .

He suddenly realized that there were still two lines of inquiry which he could legitimately and defensively pursue. Even if neither should now prove to be of any account, it was as well to remember the old Mallorquin saying: Never rush, leave yourself time to enjoy tomorrow. Who knew but that tomorrow might not bring something which would delay or even deny the inevitable?

He ate a meatball and for the first time became fully conscious of how tasty were each of the dishes. It might perhaps be an idea to have a second helping . . .

Alvarez, standing by the side of his desk, stared down at the ringing telephone. Even though it was Saturday, the

caller was likely to be Salas, demanding a report on the trip
to Barcelona.

He left and went downstairs, past the duty cabo, and out
into the road. He walked up the shaded side to the square
and unlocked his car, switched on the fan to cool the interior.
As he waited, he stared resentfully at the tourists who sat
at tables set outside the three cafés which fronted the square.
All they were interested in were beach and booze. Not one
of them would give a solitary damn if Alma were convicted
of being an accessory to murder . . . If only he could find
proof of her innocence; if only he could forget that she had
lied about that visit to her father's house; if only life hadn't
taught him that when a person lied it was because there
was cause, and the more desperate the lie, the greater the
cause . . .

The car had cooled and he settled behind the wheel. He
reversed, turned, and drove out of the square and on to the
old Palma road. Ten minutes later, he arrived at Ca'n Pario.

'Even by local drinking standards,' said Phillipa, 'you're
early; unless, of course, you've come for merienda?'

He smiled, having learned that her sharp, biting manner
was not intended to be as discourteous as it often sounded.
'I am early, señorita, because I am here to invite you to
lunch in Palma.'

'Beware the Danaans whose hands proffer gifts . . . What
do you want from me?'

'I would like you to listen to two men.'

'Who?'

'The first is Señor Gerasimos Simitis.'

'He sounds very Levantine. I visited Rhodes in the
nineteen-twenties and had my handbag snatched. That
cured me of believing, unlike my poor brother, in the
superiority of Eastern Mediterranean civilization.'

'I doubt very much, señorita, that you risk a repeat of so
sad an occurrence if we visit Señor Simitis. He is exceedingly
wealthy.'

'You believe that to be a guarantee of his honesty?'

'It is a guarantee, surely, that he will not snatch your handbag unless convinced that it contains a great deal of money?'

'You clearly understand human nature . . . Have you had merienda?'

'I've been too busy.'

'Then we shall both enjoy it now. Sit down while I go inside and make coffee.' She went indoors.

He sat. There was a suspicion of a breeze, just sufficient to tremble the vine leaves so that the sunlight which escaped around their edges danced. Cicadas were shrilling and somewhere fairly close, perhaps in the palm tree at the end of the garden, a bird which he could not identify was singing; a cock, finding sufficient energy despite the growing heat, crowed a challenge; dogs barked; far away, so that the noise became pleasant rather than intrusive, children were shouting as they played in a pool; from much nearer came the metronomic sounds of an irrigation unit; several humming-bird hawk moths were examining flowers on a lantana bush and the beat of their wings held a note of frenzy . . . When he died, he hoped it would be out in the open, amid such a scene of beauty as this.

She returned with a tray on which were two mugs of coffee, milk, sugar, two glasses, a bottle of 103 brandy, and half a coca. 'Please help yourself.'

He took one of the mugs, added sugar and milk, cut a slice of the coca, and poured out a brandy. She gave herself a brandy at least as generous as his. 'You told me who the first man is, but didn't name the second?'

'A painter. Señor Guy Selby.'

'I've not heard of him.'

'I am told that his work is talented, but he has not yet managed to become at all well known. He is a friend of Señorita Heal's.'

'Of Alma? Breeding's an odd thing. Who would have

expected a man like Gerald Heal to have had a daughter with the natural charm of Alma? Why do you want me to meet the two?'

'To discover if you can identify one of them as the person you heard quarrelling with your brother.'

'Why should it have been either?'

'Señor Simitis would have found your brother too honest.'

'If a Levantine, that goes without saying. And Selby?'

'It would not have been a question of honesty, but of taste. Your brother did not like his paintings sufficiently well to believe they would have an immediate appeal to the general public.'

'He was very conservative in all his tastes.'

'So will you come with me to Palma to meet Señor Simitis and afterwards to enjoy lunch; and to continue from there to Costanyi?'

'Costanyi? I haven't been there in more than thirty years. I suppose I won't begin to recognize the place.'

'I think you will discover that little, if anything, has changed.'

'There's somewhere which has escaped the blight of tourism? Then let us lunch there and not in Palma.'

Alvarez braked to a halt in front of Ca'n Kaïlaria. Phillipa said: 'What an ugly, pretentious pile of a place! Presumably, the Levantine was a friend of Gerald Heal's?'

'More a business acquaintance.'

'Two of a kind. It is extraordinary how really vulgar people choose really vulgar houses to live in.'

'But Señor Heal . . . Have you never seen his home?'

'He restricted his invitations to royalty and those he thought might be of use to him.'

'He lived in a noble manor house.'

She was not to be denied. 'Then he will have succeeded in vulgarizing the interior.'

They left the car and crossed to the front door. The same

maid whom he'd met on his previous visit opened it and showed them into the large sitting-room. Phillipa, unashamedly curious, began to examine the contents and she was looking at the hallmarks on the base of a silver pheasant when Simitis entered the room. He, exhibiting perfect manners, carefully failed to notice what she had been doing.

He crossed the floor, right hand outstretched. 'Inspector, please excuse my tardiness in greeting you, but unfortunately I was in the middle of a very important telephone call and not even for you could I cut it short.' He shook hands vigorously and there was no hint in his manner that their last meeting had ended bitterly.

'This is Señorita Burnett,' Alvarez said.

Simitis turned, half bowed, switched effortlessly to English. 'Dear lady, it is a very great pleasure to receive you in my humble home.'

For a moment it looked as if she were about to say something, but for once she showed a measure of discretion and remained mute, merely acknowledging his fulsome greeting with a curt nod of her head.

'Señorita Burnett's brother was very tragically killed almost two weeks ago,' said Alvarez.

'Now I understand why the name was familiar . . . Dear lady, please accept my deepest and most sincere condolences at a time of such personal tragedy.'

'Are you a Levantine?'

The question bewildered him. 'I . . . I regret that I do not understand.'

'Were you born in an eastern Mediterranean country?'

'Indeed; in Kylos, on the pearl of an island of Saphos. Perhaps you know it?'

'No.' She gripped her handbag a shade more tightly.

His bewilderment grew in the face of such hostility, but he tried to remain the gracious host. 'Permit me to offer you both some refreshment. I have just had a couple of cases of Dom Pérignon delivered—'

Alvarez interrupted him. 'That's kind of you, but we're here to ask a couple of questions and then we have to hurry away. Did you go with Señor Burnett to look at Señor Selby's paintings?'

'I did not.'

'Have you met Señor Selby?'

'Never.'

'Then thank you for your assistance.'

'Do you mean, that is all?'

'Yes.'

His expression had sharpened and his eyes were diamond bright. 'Then I'm surprised you didn't just telephone me and so save yourself the trouble of coming all this way.'

'It's been no trouble.'

'You do understand, Inspector, I have never met Señor Selby?'

'So you've just said.'

Simitis hesitated, then reverted to his previous egregiously fulsome manner. 'Surely I can persuade you to do me the honour of staying just long enough to enjoy a little champagne?'

They left. Phillipa was silent until they were driving up to the elaborate gateway, then she said: 'Men like he always make me feel I need a bath. I suppose he's in some sort of racket—drug-smuggling?'

'I don't think so. That would be too risky. He trades in ancient works of art, almost certainly buying them from peasants who have looted ancient tombs and selling them to men with money who are prepared not to ask questions.'

'He sold Gerald Heal looted treasure?'

'A diadem, supposedly part of King Priam's treasure which Señor Schliemann found at Troy and later smuggled out of Turkey. Perhaps you know the story?'

'Of course. Justin used to dream of finding the treasure even though he really believed it couldn't still be in existence. Not because of its monetary value, of course, but its historical worth. Gerald believed the diadem was genuine?'

'Señor Simitis is a clever man and he sold it as a fake, making certain Señor Heal believed it to be genuine.'

'You're saying that he made a fool out of Gerald?'

'That is so.'

'Then even though he's a Levantine, he's clever. You believe Gerald took the diadem to my brother to ask him to confirm that it was genuine, don't you? Justin would have said immediately that it was a fake.'

'Which is why it seems reasonable to believe that it was Señor Heal whom you overheard having that row with your brother.'

'But it wasn't.'

'Indeed, señorita. And knowing it wasn't, I've been trying to identify who else it might have been. Señor Simitis might have been frightened by Señor Heal's anger on discovering how cleverly he'd been fooled and he may have tried to get your brother to moderate his judgement; if your brother could be persuaded to say it might not be a fake after all, but if it was, it was the finest he'd ever seen, then Señor Heal might not be nearly so angry because his self-esteem would be far less wounded.'

'The man I heard was not the Levantine.'

'You can be certain?'

'Quite certain.'

'His voice is very slightly accented.'

'The man I heard had a voice which was more accented.'

Alvarez drew out into the centre of the road to overtake a parked car. 'If I can remember correctly, señorita, you originally described the voice as only lightly accented?'

'Well?'

'But now . . . Well, you're saying it was more than that.'

'I'm saying nothing of the sort. It's a question of relativity. When I first described the voice as accented, my point of reference was a typical foreigner speaking English; you speak very fluent English, but your accent is unmistakable.

The man I heard had less of an accent than you. The
Levantine, however, speaks an almost accentless English—
it goes with the oily appearance. Relative to him, the man
I heard had a stronger accent. So you see, I wasn't contra-
dicting myself because I'd forgotten what lie I'd told you.'

'I could never have imagined such a thing.'

'Really? I thought it was a detective's job to regard
everyone as a liar until proved otherwise.'

CHAPTER 18

They came out of the bar-restaurante into the blazing
sunshine and crossed to the Ibiza, parked under a shade
tree. He unlocked the car and held the passenger door open
for her, went round and settled behind the wheel. 'I shall
treasure our meal here,' she said. 'I have a file of good
memories and when I need cheering up, I take one out and
enjoy it. Today is going into that file.'

'I am so glad, señorita.'

'My name's Phillipa. Señorita is for people one does not
like.'

'Or whom one respects.'

She gave her short, barking laugh. 'There's little enough
cause for respecting me. When I die, I'll not be leaving
behind anything worthwhile.'

'You will be leaving memories which others can take
down and enjoy.'

'Good God, we really are becoming sentimental!'

He was disappointed by her response because it seemed
to criticize. He started the engine, backed.

She had read his thoughts. 'I often wonder which is better,
to be taught to eschew sentiment, as we British are, or to
be taught to welcome it, as are you islanders. I suppose
that depends partially on whether one is young or old.

Sentiment's bad for the young, because it leads them into emotional thickets, but good for the old, because it comforts.'

She had not, he gratefully accepted, been criticizing him. What she'd said had been prompted by her need to live through the grief of the death of her brother on her own because that was what she had been taught to do. Thank God he was part of a family who would always share, and so lighten, tragedy!

When they reached the caseta, it was to find that Selby, who was stripped to the waist, was outside in the field, painting. He carefully did not take any notice of them, not even when they walked across.

'Good afternoon, señor,' Alvarez said.

'What the hell d'you want now?'

'First, I would like to introduce Señorita Burnett.'

'Burnett . . .' He turned and stared hard at Phillipa, palette in his left hand, brush in his right.

''Afternoon,' she said briskly.

'You're . . .'

'Justin was my brother.'

It was several seconds before he realized that some words of condolence would be appropriate. 'I was sorry to hear about it.'

'Thank you.'

Alvarez did not need to be a detective to be able to judge that they disliked each other on sight. 'Señor, when Señor Burnett came here and saw your work, what did he say about it?'

'Who says he came here?'

'Señor Simitis.'

'And just who the hell's he?'

'A dealer in antiquities who suggested to Señor Pravos, the owner of Galería Mugar, that Señor Burnett should look at your work.'

'You've been nosing around.'

'It has been necessary.'

'Why?'

'Because my brother was murdered,' snapped Phillipa.

He had not the ease of social manner to extricate himself from the position in which his crude behaviour had placed himself. Resentfully, he jabbed at the painting with the brush.

Alvarez looked at Phillipa and she shook her head. The man she had heard had not been Selby. Alvarez was not surprised.

'I'm going to go for a walk,' she said. 'In which direction is the sea? Over there?' She pointed.

Alvarez waited for Selby to answer, then said sharply: 'Well?'

'Goddamn it . . . The dirt track which goes past the house leads to the cliffs.'

'Thank you,' she said, using politeness as a way of castigating his bad manners. 'I won't be long.' She went down to the track, turned left, and marched on and out of sight, a stoutish, shapeless figure who carried with her an air of indomitable determination.

'Now, señor,' said Alvarez, 'perhaps you will tell me what Señor Burnett thought of your paintings?'

'Christ! How am I supposed to work with these constant interruptions?'

'Until the murderer is discovered, I am afraid you will have to find a way.'

'Because you're so thick you think I had something to do with it?'

'You are the only person with a motive for both murders.'

'What motive had I for killing that stupid old buzzard?'

'You are, perhaps, referring to Señor Burnett?'

Selby realized that yet again he'd allowed his tongue too much freedom. 'He didn't know a damn thing about modern art.'

'Would you hold that to be cause enough to justify his murder?'

'No, I bloody well wouldn't. I didn't kill him.'

'Yet because of him, you lost the chance of an exhibition at a very important gallery.'

'He didn't know anyone had painted anything worthwhile after the end of the eighteenth century. He wouldn't begin to understand what I was trying to do and there was as much point in him trying to evaluate my paintings as there would be in you doing so. But just because he was biased, ignorant, and had a totally closed mind, doesn't mean I bloody killed him.'

'If he'd recommended your paintings, the gallery would have exhibited them. Had they done so, you might well have begun to find commercial success. Then you wouldn't have had to rely on someone else to keep you.'

He threw palette and brush to the ground. 'Alma doesn't bloody well pay a peseta towards my keep.'

'Who does, then?'

'Back home, I worked as a waiter, a barman, even a bloody doorman, to make enough money to come out here and paint, because that's all I've ever wanted to do.'

'And you still have plenty of capital left?'

'That's none of your goddamn business.'

'On the contrary, it has become my business because if I find that you have spent nearly all of it, then clearly your need to find more elsewhere is urgent; your resentment at losing the possibility of an exhibition in Barcelona must have been much more acute; your bitterness when Señor Heal reneged on his agreement would have been much stronger; and your relief much greater when Señor Heal died before he could change his will, disinheriting his wife and Señorita Alma.'

Selby was about to answer when they heard a car. A white Fiesta, bouncing heavily on the rough track, came to a halt near the Ibiza. Alma climbed out, shielded her eyes with her hand, then hurried across. Worried by Selby's expression, she said, her voice strained: 'What's happened?'

'He's accusing me of having murdered your father and Burnett,' he said violently.

'No!'

'According to him, I'm the only person with a motive for both murders.'

'That's utterly ridiculous.'

Alvarez said: 'I am sorry, señorita, but it is not ridiculous. It is the truth.'

Selby said sneeringly: 'I murdered Burnett because he gave my paintings the thumbs down and your father because he was about to change his will and you wouldn't be able to keep me any longer.'

'But I've never kept you; you wouldn't let me do that even if you were starving.'

'How d'you get that through a foot-thick skull?'

She appealed to Alvarez. 'Please, you must believe me. Gerry wouldn't do anything so horrible. He couldn't kill someone just because that person didn't like his paintings, he couldn't have killed my father. He was almost glad when he heard Gerry was going to change his will and stop my allowance because of the contessa. Her . . . he's stupid about money. He's so much pride that he won't acknowledge that a relationship should be a partnership . . . Why won't you understand that an artist worries about art, not money?'

'Señorita,' replied Alvarez sadly, 'there was one murder which makes it virtually certain there was a second one and it is my job to identify and arrest the murderer.'

'But why come here and make such filthy accusations about Guy?'

'Only he had a motive for both murders.'

'I keep trying to tell you, it doesn't matter how many possible motives, he couldn't kill anyone. I know he can be difficult, I know the way he talks.'

Selby interrupted her roughly. 'You're wasting your time, forget it.'

'I can't! I won't! It's no good trying to pretend you're

nice and pleasant and therefore couldn't hurt a fly. You're often bloody-minded, rude, boorish. But that's because you're an artist and you hate anyone and anything that gets in the way of your art and . . . Oh my God!' she murmured, belatedly realizing what she'd just said.

Where did art cease and greed begin? wondered Alvarez sadly.

'Please try to understand,' she pleaded. A thin flutter of wind briefly twitched her dark, curly hair and she instinctively reached up to recapture a few errant strands. 'All I was trying to say was that he's only difficult because all the time he's attempting to do a little more than he can presently achieve and that means he becomes terribly frustrated. But that's not the same sort of frustration that you're talking about, the kind that would make him kill . . . Gerry was my father. I liked him, even loved him, in spite of the way he treated my mother. Guy couldn't deliberately hurt anyone I love.' She began to cry and as the tears slid down her cheeks, the harsh sunlight was refracted in them so that she seemed momentarily to be sparkling with colour.

'Señorita, if all you say is true, why did you lie to me? A person lies when there is something to hide. What must you hide from me?'

'I've never lied to you.'

'Sadly, you have.'

Determined to reassert himself, Selby said violently: 'If she says she didn't, she bloody didn't.'

'The señorita's car was at the señor's house the evening before he died. The housekeeper identified the voice of the woman she heard as the señorita's.'

'I don't care who says what, I'm telling you that Alma was here all bloody evening.'

Alvarez experienced fresh bitterness. Selby's ruthless selfishness had drawn Alma into a situation from which she could not hope to escape unscathed. 'Señor, I regret I am unable to believe you. Therefore you will give me your passport and I must warn you that any attempt to leave this island without official permission will be a criminal offence. Tomorrow morning at ten o'clock you will attend at the headquarters of the Cuerpo General de Policía in Palma, where you will be further questioned concerning the deaths of Señor Burnett and Señor Heal . . .'

'You can't!' cried Alma.

'No one can regret this more than I, señorita. But I have my duty to perform . . .'

'I swear I wasn't at Gerry's that evening. I was here.'

'Then who was using your car? Whose voice could be so like yours that Señora Anzana is certain it was you?'

She went to speak, checked the words, gestured towards Selby, who muttered something wildly. 'It was my mother.' There were many more tears as she whirled round and ran into the caseta.

Phillipa walked up to where Alvarez stood by his car. 'Oh dear, I've obviously kept you waiting. Not for too long, I hope?'

'No, señorita. It has given me time to think.'

'You see, the path took me to the top of a cliff which I recognized because of the lighthouse. It's where, very many years ago, a boyfriend and I once stood and . . . As I've said before, nothing can be as boring as an old woman reminiscing about her youth, so let's leave it. Well, what happens now?'

'We return to Llueso.'

'You gathered, of course, that the uncouth young man here could not have been the person I heard?'

'Yes, I did.'

'He has a northern accent, but that's not the kind of accent I meant.'

'I understand.'

'Then do you now have any idea who was rowing with my brother?'

'No, señorita, I don't.'

She climbed into the car and settled. She did not speak again until they had reached the road beyond the dirt track. 'Has something rather unpleasant happened? You look so . . . so bewildered.'

He answered her honestly. 'I just don't know whether it is pleasant or unpleasant.'

CHAPTER 19

Alvarez drained his glass, put it down on the desk. As a buzzing fly circled it, he came to a decision. He reached down to the right-hand bottom drawer, brought out the bottle of brandy, and refilled his glass. There were times when a man needed considerable moral support.

Ten minutes later, he spoke over the phone to the plum-voiced secretary and said he'd like to have a word with the superior chief. That, he thought as he waited, was a lie.

'I've been expecting a report from you for days,' snapped Salas.

'I arrived back from Barcelona rather late, señor, and on Saturday I had two important meetings. Yesterday was Sunday . . .'

'I am well aware of what day of the week yesterday was.'

'Yes, señor.'

'Then arrange your thoughts and keep to essentials. Can you now name the murderer?'

'I'm afraid not.'

'You assured me that if you went to Barcelona and questioned a gallery owner, you would at long last be able to solve the case.'

'The information he gave me seemed to make things clearer but . . . On Saturday afternoon I questioned another witness and her evidence has complicated everything.'

'It will not have needed her evidence for that to happen. Who is she and what's her evidence?'

'The daughter of Señor Heal.'

'Has she arrived on the island for the funeral, when that's allowed to take place?'

'The fact is, she's been living here for some time now.'

'Then why have you never mentioned her in any of your reports?'

Alvarez, all too well aware of how one wrong word could lead Salas to suspect the truth, said: 'But you have many times pointed out, señor, that there is no need to bother you with inessential details. Until now, there was little reason to suppose that her part in the case could be of the slightest importance.'

'What has changed?'

'I've learned who it was who was arguing with her father the night before his death.'

'You'd no idea she could be an important witness, yet at this late date you discover it was she who was arguing with her father . . .'

'No. I have discovered it was not she.'

'And that is important?'

'Yes, señor.'

'Then perhaps you also find it of great importance that neither was the person concerned the Duchess of Alfera?'

'It was her mother.'

'Who also was not arguing with her father?'

'Who was.'

'Her mother was having an argument with her father, the night before his death? I would agree with you, that is important. So why has it taken all this time to discover so important a fact?'

'Because she wasn't on the island at the time.'

'Who wasn't?'

'The mother.'

'But . . . but if she wasn't on the island, in God's name how could she have been having an argument with him in his house?'

'I may have put things slightly clumsily. I did not think she was on the island at the time. Perhaps it would help to explain things if I started at the beginning?'

'If that is not asking for the impossible.'

'I did learn early on that on the previous evening there had been a heated argument, but I could not determine who had been the lady concerned. But when I discovered that she was not the daughter and the mother, who wasn't on the island, was, and since Señor Heal was murdered the very next morning, if, of course, it was murder which I think one must logically accept since Señor Burnett was murdered, then surely it has to be of great importance? I hope it's all clear now?'

'I feel it will prove less wearing to answer in the affirmative.'

'So I would like to question her if I may?'

'The daughter?'

'The mother, señor.'

'You feel you need my permission to question a witness?'

'You did seem rather concerned the last time.'

'You've questioned her before? But you said you've only just discovered her identity.'

'You were concerned the last time I went to Barcelona, señor.'

'What's Barcelona got to do with the mother who's here on the island?'

'But she isn't; she's returned home.'

'To Barcelona?'

'No. That's not where she lives.'

'Alvarez, I will confess that a little while ago, I'd have said it was impossible to confuse the issues any further. That was to deny your talents. Please, in the simplest form imaginable, what is it you're asking?'

'For permission to travel to Rostagne, señor, to question the mother.'

'Granted.' The connection was cut.

Alvarez replaced the receiver. He felt proud of the way in which he'd steered his superior chief away from the embarrassing question of why, if he'd known about the heated row the night before the murder of Heal, he'd not originally reported the matter so that the daughter could have been questioned at length and in depth.

'To France? You're going to France?' Dolores stopped stirring the contents of a saucepan and used the back of her hand to wipe away the beads of sweat on her forehead.

'There are only three flights a week to Toulouse,' said Alvarez, 'but I'm in luck and there's one tomorrow. I have to change at Barcelona and it's almost a three-hour wait, but I was talking to the sargento at the post and he says that there's a very good restaurant at the airport. Their cold quail in sauce are absolutely delicious.'

'You've only just been to Barcelona.'

'I know, but this is how the case keeps going. It must be a bit of a shock, so why not let's have a drink to help us get over it?'

'Can't you see I'm busy? And there's no need for you to have one either; you're drinking far too much.'

Who was it had first said that familiarity bred contempt? He could have added that it also bred abstinence, thought Alvarez sourly.

CHAPTER 20

Alvarez drove along the undulating road in the Escort hired at Toulouse airport and savoured the green, lush fields which provided a sharp contrast to the sunburned, browned

countryside he had left. Gascony. Home of the finest gas-
tronomy in France. A Carlos I brandy was delicious, but
who would dare weigh it against a thirty-five-year-old Tre-
pont Armagnac?

He turned left at crossroads. Above all, this was the land
of space. So much space that trees grew on land which could
have produced cash crops. Here, a farmer could walk for
hundreds of metres and still own the soil over which he trod.

He reached a notice which named Rostagne, rounded a
corner, and saw, built on and around a hill, the village;
similar in form to many of the inland villages on the island,
yet even at a distance clearly dissimilar in character. He
turned right. The road became a lane, at first bordered by
trees, then by fields. He passed a farmhouse in front of
which was a large flock of ducks and he remembered something that he was astonished ever to have forgotten. Ducks
were to this part of the country what geese were to Périgord.
There were those who claimed that the livers from the
specially bred and fed ducks made goose pâté de foie gras
a second-rate dish. His mouth watered at the prospect of
finding out.

A man was working a tractor in a newly harvested field
and Alvarez stopped the car, climbed on to the verge, and
shouted across to ask where La Maison Verte was. The man
removed his beret and scratched his head. Was that where
the English lady lived? Then the house was just along the
road, on the right.

La Maison Verte was an old, one-storeyed house set in a
rising field which reached up to a small copse that crowned
a hill; since the windows and doors had been painted a light
blue, the bricks were a quiet red, and the tiles a grey-brown,
the name had become a misnomer. On the left of the track
up were several long rows of lavender bushes and the air
was scented by these.

The land on which the house was set was level and he
parked in front of the garage. As he crossed towards the

front door, this was opened by a woman. He'd built up a mental picture of Tracy Heal. Alma in twenty-five years' time. Dark, curly hair beginning to silver, the attractive, unusual face matured, perhaps the inner strength slightly more apparent, the same overall impression of sympathetic understanding. Only the strength was there. Tracy's face was more immediately and conventionally attractive, sharp, and she had used considerable make-up to try to hold back the years; her clothes were designed for fashion, not comfort; her stylish shoes had heels so high that they were absurd in the countryside and Alma would never have worn them; her face expressed a self-centredness not seen in Alma's. 'Madame Heal?' he asked in French.

'And you're the Spanish detective. Are you on your own?'

'I thought it best.' He should, of course, have contacted the French police and obtained their permission for this meeting, but then a local detective would have accompanied him and everything said would have been known officially. He still hoped against hope that he was going to learn something that would enable him to bring the case to a conclusion without publicly having to involve Alma.

'Presumably you're not intending to stand there for the rest of the day?'

He followed her inside and was unprepared for the violence of the contrasting colours with which the beamed sitting-room, with open fireplace, had been decorated and furnished. She noticed his expression. 'Michel Rimaux at his most innovative,' she said dismissively, bored by the necessity of having to enlighten a pedestrian mind.

He supposed it was because of his stolid peasant background that he far preferred colours which soothed rather than jarred.

'D'you want something to drink?'

'Thank you, that would be very nice . . .'

'Have you ever had Floc?'

'I don't think so.'

'It's the local apéritif, so you'd better try it.' She turned, crossed in front of the fireplace to the far doorway, went through.

A very determined woman. One who would bitterly resent being disinherited. He sat on a chair covered in a bright yellow material and looked round the room. There were three paintings, in which everything was distorted, set in luxuriously sized and styled gilt frames, many silver knick-knacks of no practical use on the mantelpiece, and a glass-fronted display cabinet filled with figurines; the multi-coloured curtains looked hand-woven, the carpet could have hung on a wall as a tapestry of futuristic design. She was clearly a woman who spent money freely.

She returned with a tray on which were two crystal glasses set in delicate pewter stems. He took one, thanked her, drank. 'It is delicious.'

'I like it.' There was therefore, her tone suggested, no room for any guest's disliking it. 'Well, why are you here?'

'I am investigating two murders which have taken place . . .'

'Good God, man, I know all that!'

'Presumably your daughter's phoned and explained things?'

'She's tried, but she's useless at explaining, especially where a man's concerned.'

'You refer to Señor Guy Selby?'

'Naturally. I don't suppose you can explain how, after bringing her up to have the tastes of a lady, she can see anything in a lout like him?'

'I have been told that he is a good artist who may well develop into a great one.'

'If he paints a second Last Judgement, it won't make him any more socially acceptable; you can't make a silk purse out of a sow's ear, even if you feed the pig on truffles. After meeting him, I asked Alma why she'd picked on a man who's both a boor and a bore. If one has to go slumming, at least try to do it with some style . . . I expect you smoke?'

'Indeed, yes, but permit me to . . .'

'There are some on the table. You can give me one.'

She might have been brought up in the finest society, he thought, but it seemed she'd never been taught to say 'please'. After carrying the brass cigarette box across to her, it became clear that neither had she been taught to say 'thank you'.

She drew on the cigarette, blew out the smoke. 'As far as I could understand from Alma, you're here because of the row I had with Gerry?'

'That is so.'

'What about it?'

'I would like to hear what it was about, what effect it had on the señor . . . All that sort of thing.'

'All that sort of thing,' she repeated in sneering tones. 'I suppose you imagine that because I had a row with him, I murdered him. Well, there were times enough when I'd have liked to have done just that.' She drained her glass, looked across. 'You're a very slow drinker.'

'I was just . . .'

'Drink up.' She waited impatiently, then took their two glasses to refill them.

After handing him back his glass, she sat. 'Did you ever meet him?'

'No, I didn't.'

'Then you missed a real bastard, figuratively as well as literally.' She drank deeply. 'There's something which mystifies me. Just how in the hell did I ever come to marry him? I wasn't all starry-eyed, like my daughter, and I knew men professed eternal love only when they couldn't get a woman into bed in any other way . . .

'He'd charm. By God, he'd plenty of that when he thought it worth his while to exercise it. And a really sharp sense of humour. He used to mock people and always hit a painful spot dead centre. When I met him, he'd money; nowhere near as much as later on, but enough to dress in decent suits, drive snappy cars, patronize the right restaurants. He'd an air about him. When he said jump, even a head waiter jumped and it takes a good man to make them shift. But his god was ambition and he'd nothing but contempt for people he'd stepped on on his way up. I sometimes think that maybe it was the challenge that really attracted me. Even sensible women are supposed to be masochists who yearn for the challenge of rescuing men from their degradations: the drunkard from his drink, the womanizer from his women, the cad from his caddishness . . .

'He saw personal relationships in the same light as business ones—you either broke your competitor or were broken by him. But I wasn't going to be broken, so married life was one long fight. I'm a good fighter.'

It seemed he was expected to comment. 'I'm sure you are.'

'That's why he respected me. He'd married me for a background—I gave him a touch of class—but I made him respect me.' She drained her glass. 'I knew he was rolling every female fool enough to fall for his charms, but I didn't create scenes, I gave him the refined ice-box treatment. Once I told him I wasn't sharing my bed with a man who hadn't enough taste even to keep his screwing up-market. Did that make him furious!' She stood, crossed to where he sat, and held out her hand. 'You're the slowest drinker I've met for a long time.'

He emptied his glass, handed it to her. He watched her walk to the doorway and noted the care with which she moved. At a reasonable guess, she'd been drinking before he'd arrived.

She returned and sat without handing him his glass and he had to go and collect it from her. 'Did you separate some time ago, señora?' he asked as he returned to his chair.

She shrugged her shoulders. 'God knows! Sometimes seems a lifetime, sometimes seems like yesterday. The final act was when he decided he'd prefer the company of a woman whose daddy had gambled away the estate. Twenty years younger and all mincing affectation, but she was Lady Mary something or other and his Valhalla was filled with the noble aristocracy.'

'What happened?'

She laughed, with little humour. 'It was like a French farce. He went to Miami on a property deal that went sour and came back suddenly. He found Lady Mary in bed with a plain Miss. It wasn't the lesbianism that disgusted him, it was the common touch.'

'After you'd separated, he made you an allowance?'

'You think I'd have let him get away without? I'd have had the lawyers on to him in a second and they'd have blackened his image until he'd have looked more at home in a loin cloth. He knew that and since he was still in business, he didn't dare take the risk.'

'But recently he'd decided to remarry, after obtaining a divorce, and both you and your daughter were to be cut out of his will and, I understand, your allowances were to be stopped?'

'Because that's what the bitch of a contessa demanded. She'd got him by the short and curlies because of her title. Men always want more. He could buy almost anything a man could wish for, so he yearned for something money can't buy—background, breeding, the *je ne sais quoi* which separates the gentleman from the herd. Since he couldn't buy it, he tried to do the next best thing: associate with it. Contessa Imbrolie. I always think of her as Contessa Bogie. She gets up my nose. Have you met her?'

He shook his head. 'She left the island to return to her home in Italy.'

'I can picture her down to the last plunge of a neckline that in all decency and respect for age should be feet higher. Maybe it's a pity he didn't live to marry her. He'd have found out what a real bitch of a wife is like.'

'You did know that when he remarried, you were to be cut out of his will?'

'Alma told me. It didn't seem to matter to her, but then she's never been serious about money. The young of today can be such fools. It was largely her fault, I suspect.'

'How was that?'

'Because she moved in with an artist from a back-to-back background who hadn't two pennies to rub together. If that sort of thing amused her, why didn't she have the sense to keep the news to herself? She knew her father. Gerry jumped on top of any woman who'd open her legs, but he demanded that his females led the lives of Cæsar's wife; or the life that Cæsar thought his wife was leading. He wanted his daughter to stick to men who moved to Eaton Square via Eton. What did she expect would happen when she turned up with someone who was straight out of *Coronation Street*? He was so furious that he listened to all Contessa Bogie had been demanding. D'you know what message he sent through Alma? It was time we learned to stand on our own two feet. Christ, I could have—'

'Killed him?'

She drank. 'I've already answered that. And yet . . . Give me another cigarette.'

He crossed to the table and picked up the box, handed it to her, helped himself to a cigarette before replacing it. 'When you went to the island, was it to try and persuade him to change his mind?'

'I said that if he carried out his threat, I'd make him regret it.'

'How did he react to that?'

'The bastard laughed. Said he'd bought the best possible advice and there wasn't any way either Alma or I could ever get our hands on a single penny more of his. He jeered at me . . . How well do you understand people?'

'Occasionally, señora, I manage to do so.'

'Then you'll appreciate that for him our relationship was

always a battle. He had to prove that he was stronger than I. So all the time I fought him, he hated me for denying him his triumph, yet he had to respect me. But when he boasted that I'd never get a penny more of his, I . . .

'The most vicious thing about money is that it rusts away one's self-respect, but one doesn't realize that until too late. It wasn't as if I were facing penury. I've some money of my own and I could hope to find a job where languages and maturity count for more than youth. But I've grown so used to eating at the best restaurants, wearing fashionable clothes, living where and doing what I want, that all the strength had been rusting away. Instead of telling him to go to hell, I began to plead, to try to trade on our past life together. I demeaned and betrayed myself. But a strange thing happened. He didn't answer me with contempt, he answered me with sympathy. Perhaps he'd been wrong in listening so uncritically to the contessa; the past grew responsibilities that should always be honoured in the future. I expect you can guess why he acted like that?'

'No one's ever totally rotten, señora, and your admission that you could fight no longer called on his sympathies. It's even possible that had you not fought him so hard when you were together . . .'

'What in the hell are you talking about?'

He said, flustered: 'But you asked me why he was sympathetic instead of bullyingly triumphant . . .'

'In truth, you don't know a damn thing about people. You're soft-centred, always looking for the happy ending. He could always produce the charm when he wanted, just like turning on a tap. And he was so good at it that he actually had me—me, his wife, who knew exactly what kind of a bastard he was—believing that here was one leopard who'd actually changed his spots. He took me out to the best restaurant on the island, complimented me on my clothes, mentioned a little diamond clip in a jeweller's in Palma that would suit me perfectly . . . I was staying in a hotel near Alma, but in a hell of a lot more civilized area. When Gerry suggested coming up to my suite for a last drink, I agreed. How d'you like this, Contessa Bogie? . . . He'd read me like a book. There was I, responding to his charm, believing that after all he'd behave like a gentleman instead of his more normal self, offered a chance to make a tart out of the Contessa Bogie . . . How he'd been laughing to himself! Making a fool out of two women at the same time as he pleasured himself . . . Later, he became bored so he cut things short. Told me he'd been thinking things over and had decided to leave everything as it was and goodbye . . . What I'm asking you is how can any man be such a pure-bred bastard as to lead me on simply for the pleasure of kicking me back in the mud?'

'I cannot begin to understand such a person.'

'Then you're not much of a detective, are you?' She had begun to slur the occasional word.

'Was this before or after you went to his house?'

'Before. Why d'you think I went there?'

'I'm not certain.'

'Tell the truth and shame the devil. Like the bloody fool I can be, I was still hoping to salvage some self-respect. In the event, I lost my temper and behaved like a fishwife and that made him even happier because he's always been envious of my manners; mine come naturally, his called for very hard work.'

'Do you know what the time was when you left his house?'

'What does it matter?'

'It might be important.'

'Nothing's important. Drink up.'

'I think I've probably had enough.'

'Good God! Are you a man or a TT mouse? Don't they teach you to drink in Mallorca?'

'Señora, regretfully, I have a job to do. So if you would just tell me . . .'

'Certainly I'll tell you. But if I don't particularly want to be bothered to do something, I don't do it unless I'm charmed into it. So if you want to continue with such a boring subject, you'll have to charm me. And that means that first you get me another drink.'

He stood. She was at the awkward stage of drinking and if he wanted further cooperation he needed to humour her, even if to do so might result in her becoming confused.

'The bottle's on the table in the kitchen,' she said, as she handed him her glass.

'Where is the kitchen?'

'Into the hall, down the passage, and the second room on the right.'

The kitchen seemed to be equipped with every labour-saving device that had ever been invented. As he refilled their glasses, he wondered if, since she often ate out, she used half of them. He returned to the sitting-room.

He sat. 'You had this row on Thursday night . . .'

'Do you think I'm the complete bitch? A lot of men do.'

'Then they are very stupid.'

'Excellent! My soft-centred detective from Mallorca has hidden talents. I think that when you really want, you can probably be charming. Where shall we go to eat?'

'To eat?'

'If you're to charm a lady effectively, you have to take her out to dinner in a candlelit restaurant when you can murmur sweet compliments between sips of champagne. I think the Auberge du Mail. Michelin has not yet discovered that they should be awarded another two stars and so the chef is still trying desperately hard.'

'I don't think I have the time . . .'

'You want to know when I left Ca'n Heal? . . . Imagine a man so presumptuous that he names his house after himself. It would have been a coat of arms next.'

He drank.

'Charm me, I said, not bore me with silence. I can't stand silence.'

'I'm sorry, but I was thinking how sad a life you've had and how you deserve something infinitely better.'

'Speak on, O charmer!'

They left the restaurant and walked slowly across to the hired Escort, their arms linked and neither of them quite certain who was gaining support from whom. Alvarez searched his pocket for the keys, finally found them. He unlocked the passenger door and held it open for her.

'If a man has manners,' she said, 'it doesn't matter if he has a face like Quasimodo's.'

Did that mean she thought he looked like Quasimodo? He settled behind the wheel and she rested her arm along the back of his seat so that her fingers brushed his neck. 'It's a long, long time since I enjoyed a meal so much,' she said.

'It was truly delicious.'

'I wasn't talking about the food.'

Despite all the wine, champagne, and armagnac, she was not slurring her words any more than she had been much earlier; for his part, he no longer gave a damn what Salas's reactions might be when he saw the cost of the meal on the expense sheet.

He drove carefully, very conscious of her fingers on his neck. Did she realize they were tracking his flesh, sending shivers down his spine? . . . They left the road and drove up to her house. 'It's been a wonderful evening, Tracy.'

'Yes, it has.' Her fingers became more active.

'But now I must be on my way after asking a couple of questions I should have asked earlier . . .'

'Which I will answer once we're sitting down and enjoying a last drink.'

'I don't think . . .'

'Good. At this time of night, no one should think. Come on.'

He followed her across to the front door and watched her open her crocodile handbag for the key. She would never

see forty again, or perhaps even forty-five, but her figure
could have masqueraded as thirty. She'd changed into a
cocktail dress before they'd gone out and this fitted her with
seemingly artless perfection and her small breasts were
tastefully outlined . . .

'You've gone silent again,' she said as she opened the
door, stepped inside and switched on the hall light. 'What
are you thinking?'

'That I shan't be sorry to get to bed.'

'I should hope not.'

He wished his mind were not so salacious that he read into
her words an inference that could not have been intended.

They went through to the sitting-room. 'There's only one
thing we can possibly drink now,' she said. 'I have a bottle
of special armagnac that is kept for special guests on
special occasions.'

He watched her leave the room and again noted the grace
with which she moved. Earlier, she had spoken of a leopard
changing its spots; there was much of the powerful, sinewy
grace of a leopard about her.

She returned with two balloon glasses, well filled, and
handed him one. As he warmed it in his hand, he said: 'Will
you tell me now . . .'

'No, my dear soft-centred but very persistent Inspector,
I will not tell you now. One drinks armagnac of this quality
with fitting reverence, not as an irrelevance.'

'But I have to know . . .'

'And so you shall, in good time.'

'The trouble is . . .'

'You're troubled?'

'The hotel doesn't have a night porter and they said they
always lock all doors at midnight.'

'What a second-rate place you're staying at . . . So you
can see no alternative to leaving here very soon?'

'I'm afraid not.'

'What a plebeian lack of imagination!'

CHAPTER 21

Alvarez awoke in bed to find he was on his own. He stared at the ceiling. Even at his age, life could still play a joker.

Tracy came through the doorway. She was wearing a flimsy nightdress which revealed broad vistas yet provocatively concealed details. 'If sound sleeping is a sign of a good conscience, you're a candidate for sainthood.' She climbed on to the bed and pulled back the sheet. 'And yet, like St Augustine, I see you're not ready for that blessed condition quite yet.'

They sat on either side of the table in the small dining-room and breakfasted on warm croissants, salted butter from Normandy, wild strawberry or black cherry jam, and coffee. She ate the last piece of croissant on her plate, looked across. 'You're sure you can't stay for a few days?'

'I'm afraid I must get back.'

'It's probably as well.' She saw his expression, reached across the table and briefly put her hand on his. 'Surely you've learned that while sorrow can last a lifetime, happiness never outlasts days? We've both had a wonderful surprise; let's always be able to treasure it. If you stayed too long, I'd sooner or later bitch and then you'd remember me as you first imagined me to be and I would stop seeing Lochinvar . . . Much kinder happiness cut short than destroyed.'

'That's being horribly pessimistic.'

'Have you spent your life an optimist?'

He shook his head.

'Of course not. Only fools are lucky enough to be optimists . . . When do you have to leave?'

'I need to be at the airport by five-thirty.'

'We'll lunch here so that you can discover that when I
say I'm a wonderful cook, it's not just an empty boast.
Gerry used to say . . . Goddamit, why do I have to bring
his name up?'

'If you hadn't, I'd have had to.'

'Those bloody questions! D'you still think I murdered
him?'

'If he'd been killed with a knife in the middle of a violent
row, I might; but his death was plotted by someone cold
and calculating and therefore not by you.'

'I suppose I can accept that as a sideways compliment . . .
What are the questions and then for God's sake let's forget
him and think only of ourselves until you have to leave.'

'Do you remember what the time was when you left Ca'n
Heal on that Thursday evening?'

'No. But I may be able to find out.'

'How?'

She said, for once speaking almost hesitantly: 'I keep a
diary and have done ever since I was young. But at the
beginning of the new year, I burn last year's diary so that
I never have to relive all my mistakes. Does that make me
quite crazy?'

'Only very lonely.'

'You bastard! You really know how to go for the jugular.'

'I'm sorry . . .'

'Don't be, so that I can remember you as the only man
I've known who tells the truth.' She stood, left.

He stared out through the window at the land which
sloped up to the trees which covered the crown of the hill.
There'd been a fierce desire on his part to stay for the few
days she'd suggested, but some instinct had urgently warned
him not to. A similar bitter pessimism to that which ruled
her life?

She returned, a large cloth-bound book in her right hand.
She sat, opened the book at an embossed leather marker,
turned back several pages. 'Thursday, the sixteenth—that's

the day, isn't it? I'm not going to read out most of what I wrote because I need to keep some shreds of pride . . . I drove over to Ca'n Heal, lost my temper, had a flaming row with the bastard, then drove straight back to the hotel. I wrote up the diary almost immediately after returning and the time was ten-thirty, so I suppose I left him at about nine-thirty. Now, is there anything else you want to know?'

'Did you see Señor Heal on Monday the thirteenth?'

She turned back more pages, read. 'In the morning, yes.'

'When?'

'Does it matter exactly when?'

'It could be very important.'

'Damn it! . . . All right. He spent Sunday night with me, at the hotel, left after breakfast and didn't come back until the evening.'

'He was with you Monday evening?'

'All night.'

'You're absolutely certain of that?'

'How many more times d'you want me to tell you?' Her voice had sharpened.

'What sort of state was he in on Monday when he returned?'

'More bloody-minded than usual.'

'Did you gather why?'

'He mentioned something that had happened; I've forgotten what it was.'

'Try and remember.'

'What the hell does it matter now?'

'It does.'

Her expression became sullen. 'Give me some more coffee.' She pushed her cup across.

He filled her cup with the last of the coffee in the pot.

She added sugar and milk, suddenly said: 'I'm sorry, I'm bitching sooner than even I expected. But I don't want to go on and on talking about him; I want to forget he ever existed. I want to enjoy the few hours we've left together.'

'Remember what happened and then you can and will.'

One croissant remained in the wicker basket and she picked it out and put it on her plate, but instead of eating it she began to pluck off pieces which she teased between forefinger and thumb. 'He'd had a row with someone. Half life's about rows, isn't it?'

'Who was the someone, what was the row about?'

'I don't suppose he ever said. All that's certain is, he didn't get his way. There was never any mistaking when that happened.'

Alvarez sat in the upstairs restaurant in the old terminus at Barcelona airport and stared out through the window at a plane that was taxiing ready to take off. The quail were delicious, but he wasn't concentrating on them as he should. Coincidences bedevilled most investigations, largely because it was often difficult to identify them correctly. Investigators were by training loath to accept coincidences, preferring a definite and deliberate linkage to relate two events; but they happened. So on that Monday morning, coincidentally Heal might have had an argument which ended in his failing to get his way with someone other than Justin Burnett. But . . .

CHAPTER 22

'Enrique,' said Dolores, 'you're not eating.'

He started.

'Is something wrong?'

'It's just that I was thinking.' He stirred the hot chocolate, dunked a piece of coca in it.

'Ever since you returned from France, you've been thinking.'

'There's small wonder in that!'

She couldn't make out whether his thoughts were pleasant or unpleasant since one moment his expression suggested the former, the next, the latter. Was it, or wasn't it, that foreign woman again? Despite his denials, was he in fact still lusting after her?

Jaime came into the kitchen. He yawned.

'You're going to be late for work,' Dolores said.

He crossed to the table and cut himself a large slice of coca. 'It's going to be a scorcher today, you mark my words.'

She was grateful for the chance to vent some of her angry frustration. 'My husband is brilliant! In the middle of July, when there has not been a cloud in the sky for weeks, when it is like a furnace even before the sun rises, he can foretell that it is going to be a hot day!'

'All right, all right, I was only remarking. What's suddenly got you all fired up?'

'Men.'

'Where would you be without us?'

'Much happier.' She picked up her purse from the table. 'I need to buy some meat from the butcher since I have two men who demand hot food every day because they do not have to do the cooking. Make certain that whoever's the last to leave, locks up. If either of you can remember anything that long.' She left the kitchen, head held high.

'The hot weather always gets her like this,' said Jaime, as he cut himself another piece of coca. 'I mean, what's she really got to complain about?'

Alvarez nodded.

'You're in a talkative mood. I must say!' He ate. 'Well, I suppose I'd best get a move on. It's rush, rush, rush, all day long. Doesn't give a man time to live.' He stared at Alvarez. 'At least for some it's rush. For others, it's sit on their backsides and get paid for it.'

Alvarez finally spoke. 'What's that?'

'Nothing, mate; just sweet bloody nothing. But if you don't move soon, you won't get to the office before it's time to come back for lunch.' He left the kitchen and a moment later there was the sound of the front door being shut with unnecessary force.

Alvarez emptied the last of the hot chocolate from the jug into his mug, lit a cigarette. He sighed. No matter how much it further complicated the present complications, no matter that it would probably lead him along paths he feared to tread because of where they must lead, he was going to have to accept that on that Monday morning Heal had quite definitely been the man who had rowed with Burnett.

Surely Phillipa must have recognized his voice, however heated he'd become? And even if one were somehow able to accept that under extreme emotion he might have sounded very different from normal, there was no way in which his voice could have gained a foreign accent. She had been lying throughout—a fact confirmed by the way in which she had originally claimed the voice she'd heard had been very lightly accented, then had changed that description when asked if Simitis could have been the man.

Why should she have lied? To protect Heal? When she'd always despised him because he was so pretentiously false? An emotional attachment? To ask the question was to realize it was ridiculous. Could her motive have been financial—blackmail? Over what? In any case, blackmail was one of the more filthy crimes and she respected old-fashioned honour. Bribery? Virtually the same answer. There seemed to be no feasible motive for her having lied, which strongly suggested that she had not. But the premiss was that she must have done . . . She'd been mistaken, rather than had lied; an old woman, slightly hard of hearing, the foreign accent existing only in her mind. She had heard Heal, but not clearly enough to be certain and a false accusation would be an iniquity, however much she disliked the man. Heal had rowed violently with Burnett, left when Burnett refused to misidentify the fake, and that night had . . . That night he had been with Tracy . . . Alvarez hastily moved his thoughts on. Heal could not have murdered Burnett. Which reintroduced Alma and Selby . . .

'It seems,' said Salas over the phone, 'as if you have actually managed to make some progress.'

'Unfortunately, señor, I am not so certain that I have.'

'You are heir to one of your many hunches or are reluctant to discern order beyond the chaos?'

'I don't think things can be as straightforward as they're beginning to look. Assume the murderer was Selby. Alma Heal must . . . Well, at the very least she must have known of his guilt. She would have been in a terrible state—her father murdered by her lover. In that case, her mother would inevitably have appreciated that something terrible had happened to her daughter and when she heard about her husband's death she would have guessed what. Would she then have given her husband an alibi for Burnett's murder when to do so must make it that much more certain that Selby would be accused?'

'With more experience, Alvarez, you would know that women are strangers to logic. You will bring in Selby for questioning.'

'But, señor . . .'

'And the daughter.'

'I appreciate that the evidence suggests she must have known what was happening, but I'm sure she didn't. And if she didn't . . .'

'Clearly, it is not only women who are strangers to logic. Equally clearly, you also suffer from an extremely restricted memory since it's only a moment ago that you were saying the daughter must have known of his guilt.'

'Only if one assumed Selby was the murderer.'

'An assumption which comes easily. Clearly it was she who made the telephone call which drew Heal up into the mountains when he should have been seeing you. You will bring them both in tomorrow morning. Is that perfectly clear?'

'You don't think it might be an idea to wait . . .'

'Prevarication is the last refuge of the incompetent.' He cut the connection.

Alvarez slumped back in the chair. He'd tried, but this was the end of the line. As, of course, it should be. Two cold-blooded murders. If Alma had been some hard-bitten female, would he have hesitated about arresting Selby? What kind of detective allowed his personal emotions to guide his actions? (What were his emotions? He had, now it must be admitted, initially fallen in love with the daughter. He had gone to bed with the mother. It sounded like incest. Mother of God, a man could unwittingly complicate his life!) He was betraying his duty all the time he refused to accept the truth . . .

And yet . . . Strip away all emotions and become a proper detective. Phillipa had not been mistaken, she had lied. One lied when there was motive to do so. What had been her motive? It surely could only have been the money she would inherit under her brother's will. But this, by extension, was to name her the murderer of her brother and, since everything pointed to the fact that the two murders were linked, the murderer of Heal as well. Her only motive for the latter murder could be that Heal knew that she had murdered her brother. Knowing this, would Heal have remained silent—why defend someone he must guess disliked him? And would he have allowed himself to be lured up into the mountains where it would be much easier to murder him . . .

This was to heap absurdity on top of absurdity. So back to the beginning and accept only what was known to be true. Phillipa was a woman of old-fashioned standards who had loved her brother. Then nothing could or would have induced her to murder him. Further, she would do everything within her power to bring his murderer to book. She

had heard Heal have a very heated row with her brother in
the morning, her brother had been murdered that night;
every tenet of logic must suggest to her that Heal was the
murderer. Her every instinct would have been to denounce
Heal, not protect him by lying. That lie made nonsense of
everything . . .

Suddenly he realized that if it made nonsense of everything, it must make sense of something. She had lied in
order to make certain Heal was *not* arrested for murder. But
because she would never have done that had she believed
he could be the murderer, it followed that she was certain
he was not. Then she had to know the identity of the
murderer.

He parked his car and walked round to the front of the
caseta. Phillipa was not outside, but the door was open so
he called through the bead curtain.

She answered from upstairs. 'What is it?'

He moved back and sideways until he could look up
through a gap in the vine. 'It's me, señorita.'

'Thirsty?'

'I need to talk to you.'

She stared down at him for several seconds, then abruptly
stepped back to disappear from sight.

He waited, wishing himself anywhere but where he was.
She came through the bead curtain and out on to the patio.
'You may need to talk to me, but presumably you can do
that equally well with a drink as without?'

He nodded.

She returned inside. He sat down on one of the patio
chairs and thought how sad it was that in an imperfect
world it was so often the nice people who suffered and the
nasty ones who prospered.

When she came out, a tray in one hand, she was wearing
a flower-print frock, smarter than anything he had seen her
in before, and she had used a trace of make-up to very good

effect. She handed him a glass of brandy in which were three ice cubes. 'I didn't ask you what you'd like, but I imagine that you're a man whose tastes don't change.'

'I am afraid that that is so.'

'Why apologize? The world was a much happier place when there was far less change.'

'I think, happier only for some.'

'Of course. But I've learned one thing about life and because I'm old, I can say it. There will always be those who have and those who have not, whether under capitalism, socialism, communism, or any other ism. Yet the more people are fooled into striving after equality, the harsher the inequality they eventually suffer. But you haven't come here to hear my reactionary political views, have you?'

'I'm afraid not, señorita.'

'More fear?'

'Because I hate to cause unhappiness.'

'I hope you won't feel offended if I say that you really are a most extraordinary man? When I first met you—please excuse an old woman's frankness—I thought you rather dull and probably not over-bright. But as I've come to know you, I've discovered someone who knows far more about the world than most, who cares deeply about the things which used to matter, such as honesty, decency, and other people's feelings . . . Damn it, I'm sounding patronizing and that's the last thing I intended.'

'To me, you merely sound very kind.'

She stared out at her garden. 'It's no good going on trying to stave off the inevitable. You know, don't you?'

'I think so.'

'I was afraid you'd find out. If you'd been full of your own cleverness I wouldn't have been worried, but you search for the good in other people, which means that sooner or later you learn what each one of them truly is. When you know who a person really is, you know what he or she can or cannot do. When did you finally become certain?'

'I did not understand until Señora Heal told me that Señor Heal had definitely had a row with someone on the Monday morning. Unless that was an extraordinary coincidence, it meant that you had been lying when you say that the man you'd heard had definitely not been Señor Heal. But I could, of course, have guessed a long time before if I'd been clever.'

'Why?'

'There are two reasons. You said your brother had been brought up to be religious and therefore he could never have committed suicide. But he had rebelled against his upbringing since, as he saw it, it had betrayed him and therefore it was likely that he would have forsworn religion. But even if that is doubtful, the second reason is more certain. He died in the dining-room, and not the study. In the majority of suicides, the suicide takes his life in the most comfortable circumstances that his method allows. The señor would have been very much more comfortable in the sitting-room, but he chose the dining-room. Why? I think it was because of the books.'

'You're quite right, of course. He hated those books, yet he brought them out here because he didn't dare get rid of them. In them, he saw the library of our youth and the brooding authority of the father who'd made him a weak man. If it had been I, I'd have killed myself in the library as a gesture of defiance; he never could defy his father, not even long, long after his father was dead.'

'Why did he commit suicide?'

'After the car accident he suffered recurring headaches which became more and more severe. He returned to England to see the specialist who'd originally operated on him and after certain tests a tumour on the brain was diagnosed. The specialist wanted to operate and remove it, Justin refused because he was quite certain that any operation would leave him immobilized, a cabbage.'

'Then his suicide was an act of strength, not weakness.

It was not his own pain which drove him to it, it was the thought of the pain he would cause those who had to look after him.'

'I should have known you'd see it in that light . . . Ever since it happened, I've been trying to console myself with the same thought.' She closed her eyes.

'Will you tell me all that happened?'

She opened her eyes. 'There's little enough to tell. I rang him early on that awful morning because I was so worried. There was no answer. I went up to his house and let myself in and found . . . If there'd been the slightest chance of his being alive, of course I'd have called an ambulance. But it was horribly obvious he was dead.' She shivered. 'But instead of terrible grief blanking out my mind, it seemed . . . it really seemed as if someone were talking to me. With his death, all his pensions and his annuity stopped and his estate consisted only of the contents of the house and the life insurance. But life insurances contain a clause which excludes payment on suicide, so he wouldn't even be leaving that. And this voice went on to say that for years he'd been helping me directly and indirectly and all that must now stop and I'd be considerably worse off than I have been. Perhaps I'd have to leave my little house because I could no longer afford to live on the island. But with the money from the life insurance, the few years I can have left would be very much easier, not very much more difficult. I could buy some new clothes, a new refrigerator, I could once again eat out and choose the nice dishes, I could offer friends hospitality, I could go back to England to see my cousin's grandson.'

Her expression had suggested many emotions, one of which had been surprise. He judged that this had been her surprise at discovering how desperately she longed for a small touch of extra comfort at the end of her life.

'I've always been an omnivorous reader, enjoying anything well written, whether a classic, an autobiography, or

even a crime novel. It's extraordinary what arcane knowledge one can gather from books. I knew that when a gun's
fired, marks are left on the skin of the person who fired; that
an expert can tell whether a bullet came from a particular
gun; that a gun usually doesn't carry fingerprints, although
most people believe that it does . . .'

He wondered at the cold-blooded courage she had had to
show to overcome so shocking an experience. A moralist
would probably claim that greed had strengthened an
already forceful will-power; he preferred to believe it was
her knowledge that she had a right to spend those remaining
years in dignity and that there were times when a right
could justifiably be enforced by less than righteous means.

'I had to give the impression that someone had killed
Justin, then tried to hide the murder by making it look like
suicide. He'd killed himself with one bullet and because of
where he'd shot himself I was reasonably certain no one
would be able to tell whether the shot had been fired by a
right-handed or a left-handed man. Because he was left-
handed, there would be powder marks on his left hand,
but a murderer would probably not know that he was
left-handed and so would try to make it seem he'd fired the
fatal bullet with his right hand. That would mean there'd
be powder marks on both hands, but I was hoping people
would think there'd been a struggle and Justin had been
shot by the murderer who, too excited to realize that Justin
was left-handed, had tried to set the scene to make it seem
Justin had fired one shot to check the gun was working and
then had killed himself with the second one.'

'Which is what I did think.' Suicide disguised as a murder
disguised as a suicide. So cleverly carried out that if he had
not tried very hard to prove Alma innocent and had flown
to France, he would probably never have realized the fact.
'So when it became probable that Señor Heal was being
suspected of the murder, you had to deny it was his voice
you'd heard in case he was falsely accused.'

She asked, in a faltering voice: 'Have I been guilty of a crime?'

'I'm afraid you have, señorita.'

'I may be sent to prison?'

'I . . . I do not know,' he lied.

CHAPTER 23

Alvarez sat at his desk and stared at a fly which buzzed backwards and forwards along the wall and for the moment lacked the inquisitive intelligence to continue another metre to the right to find the open window. It was his duty to telephone Salas to report that it was now established that Burnett had committed suicide. But then he would not only be exposing the señorita to a criminal prosecution, he would be ensuring that even if, on account of her age, she escaped a prison sentence, her last few years would be spent in the deep shadow of not-so-genteel poverty.

Of course, if he were really honest he'd have to admit that his reluctance to telephone was not solely occasioned by his feelings for the señorita. Salas was going to ridicule his entire investigation . . .

There had never been the certainty that Heal's death had been murder, only the strongest probability that it was because it had to be directly connected with Burnett's murder. But since Burnett had committed suicide, could there be any connection? Had Heal's crash been accidental and the damage to the braking system of the Mercedes been caused by the crash, not caused it?

What possible motives for Heal's murder remained? Alma and Tracy Heal stood to gain the fortune which they had been within weeks, perhaps days, of losing. Through Alma, Selby might gain the artistic success which so far had eluded him and which, if he could not find a source of capital, might well forever continue to do so. Simitis? He had a signed receipt for a reproduction diadem and so no one could legally prove he had swindled Heal. More, had the fake diadem been the motive for the murder, it would surely have been Heal who would have murdered Simitis, having been outwitted by a man he could not legally attack? The Contessa Imbrolie? Quite apart from the fact that she had almost certainly been thousands of miles away, it had been totally in her interests for Heal to live long enough to alter his will in her favour.

So if there had been a murder, only Alma, Tracy, and Selby, had a motive. Could Alma have committed patricide or have kept silent had she known who had murdered her father? Selby, of an unattractive character but no fool, must have known that she could never countenance so despicable a crime and that if he had committed it and she had learned this—which surely she must—she would have nothing more to do with him and so the whole reason for his crime would be nullified. Could Tracy, more emotionally at risk than she would ever admit, plan so cold-blooded a murder, even if her husband had so clearly shown how he despised her?

No, none of those three could have murdered. Therefore there had been no murder, the crash had been an accident. And now he was going to have to admit that to Salas. He summoned up his courage and reached out for the telephone, stayed his hand. Once again, he was in danger of forgetting a basic rule of self-preservation. When admitting a mistake, always provide an excuse.

Heal had been very concerned over something. On that Friday morning, when waiting to be questioned by a detective—and even a man innocent of any wrongdoing suffered some apprehension in these circumstances—he had been lured away from his house by a telephone call. So couldn't it be suggested that he must have been murdered by the unknown caller for an as yet unknown motive? Salas wasn't fond of unknowns; he might well point out that Heal, arrogant and knowing he had not murdered Burnett, wouldn't give a damn about skipping an appointment with a mere local detective . . .

Alvarez leaned back in the chair. It gave a man a headache trying to sort out a confusing and confused life.

He awoke, yawned, and reluctantly accepted that nothing had changed; he was still faced with the necessity of ringing Salas. Perhaps if he concentrated on Burnett's suicide, he could divert Salas's attention away from the mistakes over Heal's accident? Then, with some degree of resigned surprise, he realized that even now he had not yet cleared up every query raised by Burnett's suicide . . .

Phillipa met him at the gate of her garden. She had changed since the morning and now wore a frock that was old and carefully darned; her make-up had weathered, adding to her years. 'I suppose you've come to arrest me? Then I'd better change out of my gardening clothes.'

'No, señorita, all I'm here for is to ask you a question.'

'Oh! In some ways, I'm sorry.' She spoke as firmly as possible, but could not prevent a slight quaver to her voice. 'The waiting is beginning to be rather trying . . . You'd better come in. Please mind the zinnia, which I was about to tie up.'

He opened the gate and stepped inside. A red zinnia with two enormous flowers had flopped and he carefully stepped over it. They sat.

'Señorita, originally, when you claimed your brother's death could not be suicide, you said that the suicide note had to be false, he could never have written it. The letter was not typed on his machine. Did you make it up, deliberately writing in a strange style?'

'Not exactly.'

'In what way?'

'I typed the note you found. When Justin bought his typewriter, he bought a similar one for me. The typefaces appear to be exactly similar, but I knew an expert would find differences. But what I wrote was correct.'

'The words were the same he had written?'

'Yes. I know I told you he couldn't have used so florid a style, but sadly that wasn't true. He so often tended to be grandiloquent, unfortunately especially when some reserve was called for. I remember that one of the few times we had an unpleasant row was when I criticized an article he'd written for laymen on Roman lamps. Another person's scholarship is really only acceptable if it's presented simply and in terms which make the ordinary reader feel he could be just as smart if he really wanted to be.'

'Then what did the message mean?'

'I don't know.'

'"But immortality can defeat death." D'you think that could be a reference to the book which the señor wrote which, I have been told, was very good.'

'A professor in America said that in his own field it was the finest work he'd ever read . . .' She stared into the distance.

He waited, but she did not answer his question. 'The translation of the Latin meant that if one sought his monument, one had to look around. What was there in the dining-room or the rest of the house which could provide that monument? Was there, perhaps, another manuscript he hoped to be even more scholarly successful than the first?'

'There was nothing like that. He hadn't written a word since he came to live on the island. Perhaps it was a reference to the letter.'

'What letter?'

'That was by the typewriter. I burned it since it probably confirmed his suicide.'

'Didn't you read it first to find out?'

'Certainly not!' She spoke indignantly. 'It was addressed to the coroner. I have never opened, let alone read, a letter addressed to someone else unless I've been given permission.'

In an odd sort of way he found that perfectly logical. Even while breaking rules most would hold to be sacrosanct, she had carefully held to others which might have seemed to be of no account. 'If that letter had merely been giving his reasons for committing suicide, it really wouldn't have been any sort of a monument, would it? That is, not one that he would want remembered for years.'

'I suppose not.'

'And why did he mention Paris? You told me he'd never been there, but might there have been a lady whom he'd never mentioned?'

'When he was young, he would never have risked Father's wrath by enjoying the company of a cocotte—had she been respectable, he'd have brought her home since Father was very broad-minded about foreigners. Once he was married, he'd never have been given the chance. When his wife died, he was too old.'

'Then why should he have mentioned Paris?'

It was some time before she answered, her mind having slipped away to other thoughts. 'I suppose it's more likely he meant the person than the city.'

'How d'you mean, person?'

'Brother of Hector, abductor of Helen.'

'I'm sorry, señorita, I do not understand.'

'They didn't make you translate passages from the *Iliad* or the *Odyssey* at school? The Trojan War. Paris was stupid enough to prefer the most beautiful woman in the world to the rule of Asia or renown in war, so he threw Aphrodite the golden apple. His reward was Helen, wife of Menelaus. When he abducted her, the thousand ships were launched and the Trojan War began. He was responsible for the deaths of so many; Hector, Priam . . .'

'Priam?' said Alvarez with sudden excitement.

'Paris was the second son of Priam and Hecuba and for

some reason was brought up by a shepherd on a hill. He married . . . I've forgotten her name—Justin would have told you immediately. But at least I can remember that you like brandy with ice.' She stood, went into the caseta.

Priam's treasure! If you seek my monument, look around you. A letter, burned before it was read. A fake diadem, supposedly from the treasure found by Schliemann and looted from Berlin by the Russians . . .

Here was another motive for Heal's death and it was because of this that he had been murdered. His murder was connected with Burnett's suicide through the motive . . .

She returned, put two glasses down on the table. 'Has something happened?' she asked curiously.

'Yes, señorita. I think that I have just learned something very important.'

'What?'

'Perhaps I might explain later, when I have thought about it more.'

She was not really interested. She drank. 'Will you tell me something?'

'If I can.'

'D'you think I'll have to share a cell? You see, I've lived on my own for so long that I'm sure I'll feel very uncomfortable if I have to be in other women's company all day and all night.'

'Please do not consider such thoughts.'

'But I must. And at my age, that sort of thing is a worry.'

'Maybe you will not have to discover the answer.'

She looked at him with a sudden, desperate hope.

He sat at his desk. Had he had a good education, he might have understood the truth a lot sooner. Or even if he had had the nous to appreciate that Burnett, steeped in the past, would tend to think in the past and would prefer sibylline riddles to straightforward statements . . .

When Simitis had decided to swindle Heal by employing

the old dodge of appearing to be the sucker, he had over-
looked one very important fact: Heal possessed the natural
gift of being able to appreciate quality. Simitis had artfully
exhibited the diadem and gained Heal's attention and later
the sale, never appreciating that Heal had instinctively
judged the diadem to be genuine. Simitis had been the fool,
not Heal, because he had not recognized the truth when it
had been in his hands.

Heal had taken the diadem to Burnett to be authenticated,
knowing that if he were right then he owned one of the most
valuable ancient artifacts in the world, as great as anything
from Tutankhamen's tomb. And if the source from
whom Simitis had bought it could be identified, there was
a chance that other pieces, or even the whole collection,
could be recovered. The fortune at stake was beyond com-
putation.

Burnett had authenticated the diadem. And immediately
there had been a violent row. Heal naturally needed the
news of this fabulous discovery to be kept secret while efforts
were made to recover the rest of the treasure; on the other
hand, Burnett wanted the kudos of becoming known as the
man who had identified the lost treasure and he didn't give
a damn what Heal stood to lose by early publication.
Heal, able to judge how weak was Burnett's character, had
threatened him with unimaginable agonies if he so much as
breathed a word to anyone. So there was Burnett with
immortality (on his terms) within reach, yet a hideous fate
(it would never have occurred to his craven soul that Heal
might be bluffing) if he reached for it.

He'd always been a coward and when a tumour on the
brain had been diagnosed, he'd refused an operation. Every
day he must have seen death closing in on him; every
day the headaches had grown more and more insufferable,
except that he had had to suffer them unless he either
submitted to that operation or committed suicide, which
needed more courage than he could find . . . More, that

was, until he realized that suicide offered him the only way
of claiming immortality while escaping Heal . . .

Alvarez parked in front of Ca'n Kaïlaria. He rang the bell
and the maid opened the door. She said that the señor was
in and showed him into the sitting-room.

Simitis, this time in a light grey suit, hurried into the
room. His manner was abrupt, not fulsome. 'Inspector, I
am a very busy man and I simply cannot accept these
repeated interruptions. I have told you all I know—'

'Not quite.'

He crossed to stand in front of the fireplace, hands clasped
behind his back. 'Does that mean that you intend to continue
with your ridiculous accusation that I cheated Gerald Heal?'

'Only that you thought you had. It took time to discover
that you hadn't.'

Simitis could not conceal his sense of shock.

'When you were offered the diadem as part of Priam's
treasure, you laughed scornfully and told the seller that this
was the hundredth time you'd been told that. But what
neither the seller nor you realized was that this time it
happened to be true. Some, if not all, of the treasure had
survived. The looters in Berlin had recognized, even if only
dimly, that the pieces were worth more than their melt-down
value, and so they'd decided to hide them, intending to sell
them as works of art when life became settled. Obviously,
they were never able to do this. Probably they were liqui-
dated. Stalin was suspicious of any Russian who'd seen the
truth of the West. The treasure was once more lost.

'Recently, at least one piece of it has been found again
and the finder, probably recognizing the craftsmanship of
the diadem but not its true history, naturally wanted as
much money as he could get and so named it as part of
Priam's treasure. Equally naturally, you derided such a
provenance and bargained until the price suited you; since
the seller believed he was lying, he was ready to accept such

a price. With the diadem yours, you set out to swindle Señor Heal . . . Only he was a lot smarter than you and became instinctively certain it was genuine. So he allowed you to think that you were fooling him, while in fact he was fooling you. Once his, he took it to Señor Burnett for authentication.

'Later, Señor Heal was in touch with you, not to boast —much as he'd like to have done—but to tell you what had happened. Señor Burnett had authenticated the diadem, but had been so excited by the discovery and what that would mean to him that he had wanted to publicize it immediately, careless of the fact that this would prevent any further pieces being bought at a fraction of their worth. He'd managed to frighten Señor Burnett into silence so effectively that the poor man committed suicide. And it seemed that Señor Burnett had left behind no word of the discovery. Speed became of the essence. Were there more pieces of the treasure extant and, if so, how to recover them before the world learned the truth?

'You were possessed by two exceedingly strong emotions and it would be interesting to know which was the stronger —your anger or your greed. You hold yourself to be the smartest of men, but had been made a fool of. If somehow this potential fortune could be all yours, you could walk with billionaires. And if at the same time you got your own back on Señor Heal, then your cup would be overflowing.

'You telephoned Señor Heal on the Friday morning and said you'd made contact with the seller of the diadem who was on the island and wanted to discuss further sales. No doubt, you gilded the lily by saying that it was certain most of the treasure was intact and that if the two of you acted very carefully, you'd be able to buy everything. Naturally, that captured Señor Heal's enthusiasm and so he saw nothing peculiar in a meeting deep in the mountains—all parties needed absolute secrecy.

'When he arrived, you drew him away from his car. My guess is, you said you were due to meet your contact off the road, perhaps in the ruins of an abandoned building. That gave your hired accomplice—you'd never find the courage to do such work yourself—time to sabotage the Mercedes.

'When no contact turned up, you said there'd been some sort of a hitch, but the other man was bound to be in touch again. Señor Heal left, frustrated, perhaps even a little suspicious of events, and in consequence of high emotions and the drinks with which you'd plied him, he drove even more furiously than usual. At one of the most dangerous parts of the mountain road the brakes failed, he went off the road and was killed. The fortune was yours and yours alone.'

'Prove it!' shouted Simitis.

'I can't.'

He stared at Alvarez, fear giving way to amazement, amazement to calculation.

'Not right now. But if I start a full investigation into all your movements, if the incoming and outgoing passenger lists of every aircraft during the relevant times are examined and your accomplice identified, if every person who was on the mountain road on that Friday is asked if he or she saw you or your car, if a thousand and one further avenues of inquiry are followed, then sooner or later I shall uncover the leads that name you the murderer.'

'*If?*'

Alvarez was silent.

'How much do you want?'

'The name and whereabouts of the man who sold you the diadem.'

Simitis's voice became scornful. 'So that you can try and get everything for yourself? You, a peasant on this flea-speck of an island, have dreams of becoming as rich as Crœsus? Take what I offer you, ten million pesetas, and continue living, in easier circumstances, the kind of life for which you're suited.'

'I'm not interested in the treasure.'

'Then why d'you want the name?'

'So that I can give it to the director of the Museum of Humanities. He can try and recover the treasure for Mallorca.'

'You must be crazy. If I pass on the name, I lose everything . . .'

'You have already. Either you give it to me or I intensify the investigation until you are named the murderer. And until your arrest, you will spend every minute of every day knowing that fate is getting closer and closer and that soon you will be arrested, tried, and be sent to prison. Think what prison must mean for a man of your refinement. How will the crude peasants of this flea-speck of an island treat so elegant a señor as you? Can you hope to survive their rustic ways? And you will not even have the consolation of knowing that when you finally leave prison—should that ever come to pass—a fortune will be awaiting you. Refuse my deal and I'll tell the world the truth and the treasure will be found by others.'

'No one will believe you.'

'They will when they examine the diadem which Señor Heal bought from you . . . Fight me and you gain nothing, lose everything; act with me and while you gain nothing, you lose nothing. As an educated, clever, refined man from the great world beyond, do you think you really have any choice?'

CHAPTER 24

Salas said over the phone: 'The two men had a fight?'

'Yes, señor.' Alvarez stared at the glass on his desk in which there still remained a generous measure of brandy, his nervousness growing with every second. He readily recognized that he was far from a clever man, yet if he were to save Phillipa from prison he now had to pull the wool over Salas's eyes—and Salas was surely a very clever man or how else could he have become a superior chief? 'Señor Burnett was a very nervous and excitable man. He owned this old revolver and produced it to threaten Señor Heal. My guess is that in his excited state he appeared far more dangerous than he was and Señor Heal, desperate to save himself, tried to gain possession of the gun and in the struggle it inadvertently went off. That was the first bullet, which hit the wall. Señor Heal then managed to force him to drop the gun. However, perhaps with the strength which comes to weak people when they are desperate, he got hold of the gun again and the struggle was resumed. Tragically when the gun was fired a second time, the muzzle was pointing at his forehead.'

'There were powder marks on both his hands.'

'He was left-handed, but he could do far more with his right hand than the average right-handed man can do with his left. His sister has confirmed that fact.'

'If that's what happened, how did the whisky get on the table?'

'As can be readily appreciated, finding himself with a dead man and remembering the violent row they had had that morning, Señor Heal panicked, believing he would be found guilty of murder.'

'Señorita Burnett denies it was he who had the row with her brother in the morning.'

'The señorita is old, a little deaf, and very stubborn. It now seems she did not hear as clearly as she has claimed. Having first denied it could have been Señor Heal's voice, she was very reluctant to admit that it might have been.'

'You still haven't explained the whisky or the suicide note. And what was the row about?'

'Horrified by what had happened, Señor Heal took the only course of action which then seemed to him to offer any chance of escaping being tried for murder. He set the scene to make it look as if Señor Burnett had committed suicide. But because he did not know the dead man, he had no idea that here was one of the few Englishmen who never drank whisky. As to the suicide note—it is meaningless. Señor Heal was a self-made man from humble beginnings who had become very rich and, like many such, he had an exaggerated respect for people of scholarship. He imagined that Señor Burnett would write a suicide note in the most grandiloquent of terms and that is why he typed what he did on his own machine—by sheer luck he had a similar one—little realizing that his choice of words made it clear that it could not have been composed by the dead man.'

'What were they arguing about?'

'A gold diadem which Señor Heal had bought and which he believed had come from Priam's treasure and therefore was very, very valuable. He wanted Señor Burnett to authenticate it, but Señor Burnett was reluctant to do so then and there. The final argument that evening, when Señor Heal had returned, was probably fuelled by Señor Heal's offering a large sum of money for an unreserved and immediate authentication of the diadem. Señor Burnett would have been outraged by such an attempt to corrupt his academic honesty.'

'Where is this diadem?'

'I expect it is either in the safe in Señor Heal's house or in a bank . . .' He stopped.

'Well?'

'I'm not quite certain how to put this, señor.'

'Rationally.'

'I have spoken to Señorita Heal about the diadem and she feels that it carries bad luck for the owner. I find it difficult to believe this is possible . . .'

'Does it matter what you believe?'

'She thinks it would be dangerous to risk such bad luck

and since the diadem is of the greatest historical significance
as well as value, would like to present it to a museum. She
mentioned that her father had so liked living on this island
that she was sure it would be his wish to present it to the
Museum of Humanities in Palma. That would, of course,
be wonderful not only for the island, but also for Spain.
However, I have the feeling that . . .'

'What?'

'If her father's name were to be blackened by a further
and prolonged investigation into the case, if too much
evidence were made public and this cast her father's image
in a dubious light, she might be far less eager to present it
to a museum here, but might well decide to present it to
one in her own country.'

There was a long pause, then Salas said angrily: 'How
can all this evidence be suppressed—well, not be published
—if Heal was later murdered and his murder was directly
connected with such events?'

'Señor, you will remember that the assumption that
Señor Heal had been murdered was largely based on the
belief that Señor Burnett had been murdered. But we
now know that Señor Burnett's death was accidental.
Further, there was never firm evidence that the car crash
had been deliberately engineered; all Traffic could say
was that the damage to the brake systems could have
been sabotage. Now that we know everything, we can for
the first time clearly see the course of events. Señor Heal
was trying to hoodwink the law and, being an intelligent
man, he would realize that if his deception were exposed
he would be under even deeper suspicion of having
committed murder. In the face of such danger, with a
mind filled with foreboding and fear, perhaps panicking,
what more natural than that he should drive even more
furiously than usual? In the mountains, that is so often
fatal.'

There was no immediate and contemptuous comment

from Salas. As the silence lengthened, Alvarez reached for
the glass.

Alvarez sat within sight of the portrait of a naked Alma,
but even more than before he took care not to look at it.
'Señorita, I have come here to explain certain facts. Your
father was present when Señor Burnett died.'
    She gasped and Selby reached out to grip her hand. 'Are
you saying . . . Are you saying he killed him?'
    'We cannot be entirely certain of some of the details, but
we can be quite sure that Señor Burnett's death was not
deliberate. The two were struggling when Señor Burnett
had his gun, the gun went off and the second time killed
him. There was no intention on your father's part to kill
Señor Burnett.'
    'And Father's death?' she asked in a whisper.
    'That was accidental. Desperately worried by the fact
that he had tried to conceal his presence at Señor Burnett's
death, and by what he had done to try to suggest that that
had been suicide, he did not concentrate on his driving. In
the mountains, tragically, that can be fatal.'
    'Both deaths were accidental?' asked Selby.
    'Officially, we will call Señor Burnett's death accidental
for the sake of the señorita. But I have to say that had Señor
Heal lived, we might well have had to charge him with
manslaughter as well as an attempt to pervert the course of
justice.'
    'That's great! Accidental death twice over, yet the last
time you were here you called me a double murderer.'
    'Certain evidence was not known then and it did
appear—'
    'Only to someone who's bloody blind. What I'm saying
is—'
    'Just for once,' interrupted Alma, 'don't say it.'
    'You expect me to listen—'
    'In silence.'

He was so astonished, he became silent.

'Señorita,' said Alvarez, 'somewhere among your father's possessions there should be a gold diadem.'

'That's a kind of a crown, isn't it? There's one in his safe.'

'That was the cause of the fatal argument; but for that, both señors would be alive today. It has also brought bad luck to other people. I am very worried that if you keep it, it will do the same to you.'

'Like the Hope diamond?'

'That sort of thing's all a load of cod's,' said Selby loudly.

'Señor, I do not think it is safe to be so quickly scornful of such things.'

'Goddamnit, this is the end of the twentieth century, not the beginning of the tenth! We've stopped believing in witches and warlocks.'

'Señorita, I have to tell you that the diadem is not only of very great historical interest, it is also very, very valuable. Now, of course, it belongs to you and your mother. I am asking you not to keep it, however valuable, but to present it to a museum. And since your father lived here on the island, you might wish to present it to the Museum of Humanities. Perhaps it seems difficult to give away something so valuable, but even without it you both will inherit a very considerable sum of money from the estate and will be able to lead comfortable lives. I am old enough to understand that moderate wealth is not dangerous to those who own it, but very great wealth is.'

Selby said: 'Her old man owned this thing which is worth a lot of money and you're suggesting she gives it away because you reckon it carries bad joss and also it's dangerous to be megarich?'

'Yes.'

'I just don't believe I can be hearing right. I mean—'

'Guy,' she said, 'dry up.'

'I'm not going to have him sit there, trying to make a fool out of you—'

'Right now, it's you who's being the fool.'

He swore violently, stood, charged across the room to go outside.

'I'm sorry,' she said.

'Señorita, there is no reason to apologize.'

'Considering he's an artist and so should be alive to all the nuances, it's surprising how blind and deaf he can sometimes be. Right now, I suppose it's because there's money involved. That always scrambles his mind . . . There's an awful lot you haven't said, isn't there?'

'Nothing of any real importance.'

'Everything of real importance, I'd say. But I really would be a fool if I ever thought you'd tell me exactly what that is.' She stood. 'You'll have a drink, won't you?'

He looked towards the outside doorway. 'Would it not be best if I left?'

'Because of Guy? He'll be back in a while, the explosion over and all calmed down. You don't like him, do you?'

'If that is true, it will be because I think he may not make you as happy as you now believe he will.'

'How sweet you can be! Mother's absolutely right.'

'Your mother?'

'I rang her to find out how she was. She talked about your visit in very glowing terms. She hopes that one day she'll meet you again.'

'You really mean it?' asked Phillipa, her voice little more than a husky whisper.

'Indeed,' answered Alvarez as he stood on the patio.

'I'm not going to have to go to prison?'

'Señorita, if you forget everything except that you are slightly hard of hearing and very stubborn, you will not go to prison and your brother's life insurance will be honoured.'

'I . . . I can hardly believe it. Oh my God, it's been a terrible nightmare and now . . . Was it all so very wrong of me?'

'Wrong means different things to different people, but I think that to you and me it means the same thing. It was not wrong of you.'

'I . . . I don't know what to say. Yes, I do! I've a bottle of Codorníu Ana I've been saving for a special occasion. We will drink it now.' She hurried into the house, flustered, far from her usual self-controlled self.

He sat down on one of the chairs and stared out at the garden and listened to the sounds of his beloved countryside. The opposite to wrong was right. There was right in the world when good prospered and evil suffered. The two señoritas, each in her own way, would prosper. Simitis would suffer, far more than if he had merely been jailed, because for the rest of his life he was going to have to live with the agonizing memory of the immense fortune which had so nearly been his, but which he had lost through his own clever cupidity. And the insurance company, called upon to pay out on a claim for which they were not legally liable? If taxes and death were two certainties in life, a third was that all insurance companies prospered . . .